Death

by

Crow

All photos are the property of the author,
or are used with appropriate permissions.
Interior graphics by Urban Fir.
Edited by Tigerpetal Press.
Cover design by Carolin Petersen

ISBN 978-0-9939361-7-3

Also by Rosemary Rigsby

Prairie Seas, Mountain Harvest
My teacher, her life, her legacy
Biography

Five Nights in a Turtle
Not Your Ordinary Hawaiian Vacation
Travel Memoir

Lewa's Birds
Feathers, Friendship, and Felony
Novel

A Legacy of Ghosts
Novel

Dedicated to…

…family and friends who have given me decades of
good reasons to visit the towns and cities
of the BC Interior.

Table of Contents

1: February: Nathan ....- 1 -

2: January: The Stable ....- 9 -

3: February: The Newbie ....- 13 -

4: January: Back Room...- 17 -

5: February: Visions ....- 19 -

6: February: Victim...- 23 -

7: January: Bookshop ....- 29 -

8: February: Dave ....- 31 -

9: January: Kitchen I..- 37 -

10: February: Pokey..- 41 -

11: February: Tracks...- 47 -

12: January, Kitchen II ....- 55 -

13: February: Dr. Brad..- 57 -

14: February: Death Wish.......................................- 63 -

15: April: Arcade ....- 67 -

16: May: Nightmare...- 71 -

17: March: Spring Break ....- 77 -

18: May: Confessions ....- 81 -

19: May: Chemistry ....- 85 -

20: May: The Trestle ....- 93 -

21: May: No Body ....- 99 -

22: May: Explanations......................................- 103 -

23: May: That's It ....- 109 -

24: May: The Right Bridge..............................- 113 -

25: May: The Plunge ....- 117 -

26: August: Crow Warning..............................- 121 -

27: August: Two Hours Earlier.......................- 129 -

28: August: Crow Summons...........................- 133 -

29: August: Death by Crow ....- 135 -

<u>Prologue</u>

Cait downshifted her borrowed truck and wheeled it off the main road into the laneway's slushy ruts. The pick-up jolted and slithered sideways. She backed off on the gas. She had news, but pitching the truck into the ditch wouldn't help share it faster.

She peered into the dusk, her breath condensing in her face. Which wasn't odd for January, but inside the cab? She wasn't about to complain. She didn't own a vehicle of any kind–she owned a horse, who lived at her mother's stable at the end of this never-ending cowpath. She had travelled this particular cowpath all her life. Was it the dark that made the trip feel longer?

She was free from the treadmill of death, aka her current job at Teagan's bookstore, and could finally announce it to the world. Mum would be glad, or so she hoped, but first, Firefly, who yes, as Teagan said, got to hear everything. Firefly could only offer sympathetic nickers while munching hay, but she always listened.

She would stroke her mare's chestnut neck and let the excitement fizz through every nerve, every rejoicing molecule. She would bury her face in Firefly's mane, a perfect place to confess her panic. Was that what the jangling in her brain was all about? The headache was back. This good news should have eased her anxiety, but maybe the combination of excitement, jubilation, and yes, terror was too much at once. But a little horse therapy would help. She would tell Firefly the job was hers. She still couldn't believe it.

The job meant moving to another city. A smaller city away from the coast, an eight-hour drive from here, but in new surroundings with new people, she could be her own person: not an only child or a student or a predictable friend or a grunt in a bookshop. People would have to take her seriously.

The truck crunched to a halt on the frosted gravel in front of the stable. Across the paddock, lights in her mother's house lured with their promise of a hot meal, but Cait stepped out into the silver semi-circle cast by the light above the stable door.

She raised her head to inhale winter air. Platinum clouds streaked a new moon. A black silhouette sailed over her head. A bat? Too noisy. No, a crow. Flying in the dark? It soared to the top of the stable and screeched a single 'caw.' Cait shivered.

<u>Death By Crow</u>

1: February: Nathan

Papers from an open folder spread across the surface of Cait's desk, rumpling against a paper desk calendar. It wasn't hers. She picked it up. What should she do with this? It just took up space. Shrugging, she circled a date and wrote on it.

A motion caught her eye, and Cait looked up, A figure stood in her office doorway. Black jeans, black jacket, black hair over his forehead. Hands in pockets, he gazed at his feet where one soot-grey boot with a shiny toecap inched over the threshold. She eased her death grip on the desk calendar and put it down. Her first consultation. She had been the new school counsellor for a whole four and a half days. *Breathe in. Breathe out. It will be okay.*

She had made it to Friday but still heard Teagan's words in her head. Or rather, everybody's words in her head. *Are you sure this is the job for you Cait? It wasn't your dream, was it?* Why did everybody assume that because she had first attempted journalism, that being a journalist was her dream job? It wasn't. It was an aspiration that seemed like a sensible choice in Grade 10. She had embraced university and entered her first internship full of optimism. Funny how that changed. 'Funny' wasn't the right word. No, being a journalist wasn't her dream. The dream came later.

The boy's foot scuffed back and forth over the threshold. Cait refocused on the present.

"Oh, you must be Nathan. Please come in." Such formality. She would have to work on that.

The boy's head snapped up and he looked around the office. He looked over his shoulder into the hall, and at the plaque on her door, which still said 'Mr. S. Goode.' He kept his hands deep in his jacket pockets.

"Where's Goode? Mr. Goode. Are you cleaning in here or something?"

Concentrating on relaxing her fingers, Cait smiled at the boy. She repositioned the paper desk calendar beyond the scattered pages from the file. She shuffled them together and closed the folder but kept one hand spread on top as if it might fly away.

Her stomach fluttered. She swallowed. "N-no, I'm Cait Lee." Should she have introduced herself as Miss Lee? Oh, well. "Mr. Goode is still unwell and won't return for some time. I'm filling in."

The human resources supervisor at the school board had hinted that the position could be permanent, not that Cait wished any permanent harm to Mr. Goode. Staff room gossip had it that he should have retired long before the incident with the crow. Whatever that was. She hadn't asked.

Nathan walked forward a few steps. "Oh. You're a teacher?"

She hoped her smile projected bright confidence. "Counsellor. Like Mr. Goode. Please sit down."

The boy dragged his feet to the chair before her desk. He flopped into it and peered at her from under the fringe of dark hair.

Stone brown eyes and his mouth like a line in cement. Her armpits prickled.

"So, Nathan." Cait covered the quaver in her voice with a throat-clearing cough. "Mr. Kinney tells me you have missed some classes."

She lifted the corner of the folder as if peeking underneath, then lifted her lips in what she hoped was a smile. Nathan looked at the snaps on his jacket. He curled and uncurled his hands on the armrests. Cait glanced at the file, then slid it to the side of her desk.

"Nathan, this isn't just about the missed classes. There's also the matter of your outbursts today."

Like throwing a chair at Mr. Grewal's blackboard and threatening poor Miss Feenwell in the cafeteria. Although drowning her in her own soup might end the blandest lunch menu ever. Discovered on day two of her new job.

Cait mentally shook herself. Considering Miss Feenwell's bill of fare was a pathetic delay tactic. She needed to concentrate on this case. Was Nathan a case? Or just a kid who had lost control? Maybe he had an argument with a friend. Or a girl gave him the brush-off. Everything was so serious at his age, which, she had read from the file, was sixteen. She cleared her throat again.

"I would like to understand what's going on. Perhaps you can tell me a little about yourself? What kind of hobbies you have."

Nathan looked up, brows a black stroke over narrowed eyes.

"Hobbies?"

"Well maybe not."

Cait's mind groped, but the words came to her unsummoned, "You're a good student. Nothing like this has happened before."

"How do you know that? You just got my file." No challenge in his voice. Just a patient curiosity as if asking her favourite colour. "Can you speed read?"

Cait tried not to shift in her seat and resisted the urge to tap the folder. At least he didn't seem surprised to hear he was a good student. Where had that insight come from? Nathan was right. She hadn't had the file long enough to read it all. And she hadn't seen this boy before.

But she could have, if she had left her office this week and had gone out to talk to the kids. She straightened her back.

"Yes. I mean no, I can't speed read, but Mr. Kinney said that throwing chairs and shouting at Miss Feenwell is completely out of character for you."

Nathan shook his head. "Wow. He got something right. But I talked to D– Mr. Grewal. I told him I was sorry. And I'll see Miss Feenwell before I go home."

"I'm sensing that you're unhappy about your loss of control."

"You sense that? Or did Kinney tell you I'm unhappy? He wouldn't know if his big toe was unhappy."

Cait worked to keep her expression neutral. "Mr. Kinney is concerned about your actions. He didn't offer an opinion on your state of mind. But you're not exactly bubbling over with sunshine and smiley emojis."

A tic in Nathan's cheek hinted at a smile.

"So," Cait continued, "if we can take a moment here, I would like to help you get back on track–"

"Back on track?" Nathan gripped the arms of the chair and half rose to his feet, like he was about to take flight. His voice rose. "What do you know about tracks?"

Her mind went blank. Face too, probably. Why so surprised about the mention of tracks?

"Nathan, it's just an expression." Had he never heard it before? Was she more archaic than she thought? Cait placed her hands flat on her desk. "Please sit down."

This one had come out of the blue. Here she was prepared to deal with career decisions or offer course guidance or emotional support for struggling students, but how to slot this case? Nathan. A good name, meaning 'given' of ancient origins. She remembered that from high school when she and her friends were obsessed with finding meanings in their names. She looked into the dark eyes that looked much older and deeper than sixteen years. He met her eyes. Was there pleading in those depths?

"Maybe you should tell me what this is really about," she said.

"Why?"

"Because I can't help you without knowing what's going on. I haven't been out of high school so long that I've forgotten how I worried about everything. How I looked. If I was liked. If I said the wrong thing. Or if something happened that I didn't understand."

"Why would you want to help me? Kinney thinks I'm a problem child. Goode agreed with him but was nicer about it."

"I could tell you that it's my job. But I've been through some weird stuff myself and maybe I will understand whatever it is that caused you to throw a chair at a blackboard."

Nathan subsided into the chair, looked at her, then shrugged. "It won't make any difference." His mouth resumed its line of bleakness. An edge in his voice rose above the air of patience. "I won't live long enough for anything I do to matter."

Cait clamped her jaw so it wouldn't drop open like the door on Miss Feenwell's black oven. She kept her voice low and steady, "Why do you say that?"

Nathan looked at her, then at a point above her head, then closed his eyes. "Because before the end of May, I'll be dead."

2: January: The Stable

Cait heaved another shovelful of manure and straw into her wheelbarrow and sneezed. Deathly cold for January on the west coast, but a lot of dust in the stable, despite the cold and damp outside. In here, it was warm by comparison and the horses, with their fuzzy coats, didn't mind. She didn't mind either and had hooked her jacket on the edge of the stall door. Cleaning stalls was guaranteed to generate warmth. And hunger. She looked forward to her mother's New Year's dinner.

Mum's stable business always needed an extra hand, especially on holidays, and she had given two of the staff the day off. Cait had come out early to help. Many of her horsey friends asked why she didn't work at the stable until she got the job she wanted. When she was a teen, her answer would have been something along the line of *would you like to work for your mother?* Now, she could easily work for her mother and help manage the business. Too easily.

She could live at home while job hunting. Or career launching. Whatever. She blew her nose. One reason for not staying here was her hay allergy, as mild as it was, but the cotton fluff of the parental nest, and the safety of her own room in the house she grew up in, would suffocate her. But with a nice degree in her pocket, she couldn't hang around waiting for calls or messages without pulling her weight. Or shovelling it. Except for the watering eyes, she enjoyed the work. Shifting bales of hay around and raking up manure was a wondrous workout. And she still had her horse.

Despite Firefly and the freedom to ride whenever she liked, the city called. She had many friends there, like Teagan, who had given her a couch along with a job. Not that shelving books there was a long-term career plan. It wasn't even a short-term plan. Teagan was already well into her long-term plan: a thriving little business in the middle of the city with a convenient apartment above it. If it weren't for Teagan, she would be serving burgers somewhere, or be stuck here at home with her favourite shovel.

Teagan had said she was welcome until she was hired for the job she really wanted. Neither of them had expected she would remain unemployed for seven months with only one inquiry in response to many applications. But that one had led to an interview. She took it as a sign although she didn't believe in omens or premonitions or clairvoyance or second-sight. That's what she kept telling herself despite the vision in the quad that had led to this torturous waiting.

The call had to come soon, and she would counsel teens in a modern high school. She would help them sort out the frustrations of being not-yet-an-adult, not yet independent, but yearning to fly. Help them set a course for their lives. Her vision. Literally.

"Cait, I heard that sneeze. Can I get you a pill? I'm going to the house to baste the turkey." Mum in the next stall, spreading fresh straw.

"Thanks Mum. I'm good. Almost finished anyway. Then I'll tack up Firefly and go for a ride in the park before dinner."

"It's icy in places. I had Arrow in there yesterday. You'll be careful?" Her mother peered through the grill between the two stalls.

"I'm always careful." Cait dropped the shovel on top of her load and put a hand to her forehead.

"Is that headache back? Maybe you should see the doctor?"

Strands of black hair that had escaped her elastic whipped around Cait's ears as she shook her head.

"Dad called." Her mother disappeared as she turned to rake. "He said the gig last night went well. He's on his way from the airport."

"I know. Saw on my phone." Cait lifted the wheelbarrow and shoved it into the aisle.

"Have you heard from anybody? About the job?"

Cait spoke over her shoulder, maybe a bit more loudly than necessary, but the wheelbarrow squeaked.

R. Rigsby

"It's only been three days. They said they would let me know within two weeks."

The consultation, even though it had been done via internet, had tested her nerves. She had forgotten the name of the lady from the school board who said they were impressed with her resume. Also, her previous experience working with young people was a big plus, as was the recommendation from the school where she had her last practicum.

Cait had tried to ask intelligent questions, like who was the principal, the vice-principal, and how many students were in the school. The principal was a Mr. Kinney. The position of vice-principal was open. There were about 300 students. The lady from the school board had been pleasant but had kept glancing at the corner of her screen. Checking the time?

The last load of dirty straw tumbled onto the heap. Cait manoeuvred her wheelbarrow back down the ramp, still thinking about that on-line meeting. She had asked if the position was a newly created opening. It wasn't but an explanation wasn't offered. Maybe the former counsellor had won the lotto. If she got the job, she would start in February.

Nerve endings tingled. Why the urgency? She hadn't felt this way since the dream. She kept calling it a dream, but she hadn't been asleep.

3: February: The Newbie

Cait wished she'd had time to read more of Nathan's file notes. When she had come up the front steps after her lunch break, Mr. Kinney had opened the door in front of her.

"I was told you had left the building," he said.

"Out for a short walk. I like the exercise and fresh air." She didn't say it was much preferrable to the stuffy staff room and some of the stuffy staff. Some had been welcoming, like Dave Grewal, teacher, and Jen Aiken, the secretary.

"I'm sure. I'm giving you this kid's file." He slapped the folder into her hand. "If I had a vice principal, I'd give it to him, but I don't, and I can't do it all around here."

Cait had read the name on the file tab but hadn't heard of the student. She must have looked inquiring, or skeptical, because Mr. Kinney clicked his tongue and recounted the student's transgressions. The unspoken transgressions seemed to include Nathan's ability to get up Mr. Kinney's nose, judging by the moustache rubbing.

On Monday, Cait had presented herself in the principal's office at eight a.m., per instructions from Ms. Human Resources. Mr. Kinney had glanced at her, furrowed his brow, and pointed to a chair. He finished hammering his computer's keyboard with a message. Or missive. Or dismissive. The frown had devolved into a scowl.

Then he had rubbed his moustache and bared his teeth at her, which she now understood was a smile, and welcomed her to Upper North High School. Mr. Kinney had done the necessary introductions and shown her to an office. The introductions didn't include a vice principal.

Reciting Nathan's misdeeds while handing off his file, was the first time since Monday Mr. Kinney had spoken to her, beyond saying good morning or good evening. He departed with, "I'm going to the cafeteria to see Miss Feenwell. She's very upset. Nathan will be in to see you. Grewal is having a chat with him, then he'll be all yours."

When Nathan had arrived at her door, she hadn't read beyond the first few pages of a rather thick folder. Was there anything about an untreatable condition or a family history of something dreadful. Did he have cancer…? No, Mr. Kinney would have told her.

Nathan shifted in his chair, and Cait took a breath, her thoughts swirling.

"Now Nathan, there's no reason for you to believe you are going to die…no disease." She bit her lip. She didn't like the return to counsellor-speak.

Nathan glared. As if she had transported in from another planet. One reserved for new counsellors who had no idea what they were doing. Or the person who had just told him she would understand had been replaced by a stiff-necked crone from the reign of Queen Victoria. She sat up straighter in her chair and Nathan slouched further in his.

"Maybe I should die. It might be better that way." He shook his head and resumed gazing down the front of his jacket.

This time Cait couldn't keep her mouth from opening to the dawning realization that she was out of her depth. This couldn't be happening. Floundering in waves of confusion, she remembered her dream, her joy on nailing this job, a chance to fly. This is what she wanted: to help teens with all their challenges. And here was a challenge. Unless he was faking it. Trying to shock her. Testing the newbie. Was that in the file?

She reached for the folder, changed her mind, and clutched the arms of her chair. Taking a breath, she rolled from behind the barricade of the desk to directly in front of Nathan. She leaned forward, hands clasped in her lap.

"Nathan, please tell me what this is about. I will listen. But I want the truth. I know when I'm being scammed."

Was he being bullied? Were there problems in his home? An abusive parent? Or siblings or step-siblings pre-empting parental preferences? He didn't look neglected. His clothes were clean, his hair shone with blue high-lights, and his colour was good. His eyes were clear, if maybe tired. Maybe haunted.

Nathan looked at his hands, again at that point above her head, then at her face.

"How old are you?"

4: January: Back Room

Cait sat on a step stool in the back room with a cup of tea. Break time. Out front, Teagan rang up a sale for the last of a steady influx of customers. It had been a busy morning. A new semester often brought in students choosing to buy their books from the shop for various literary classes, and Teagan did a nice trade in used books. Unlike the one in Cait's lap, which was new. She had spotted it that morning, out of line with its shelf-mates. She had pulled it out to straighten it, then had looked at the cover.

Cait flipped a page and placed her phone on the empty carton beside her. Useless. She shoved it out of sight behind her. Staring at it wouldn't make it ping the one message that would liberate her from this treadmill of death. Okay, it wasn't that bad. She loved books. Loved reading. And writing. Loved writing so much that she had thought she should take up journalism and write insightful reviews. That sensible choice had crashed and burned. If she wasn't the winning candidate for the counsellor job, she could keep working for Teagan. It was a great little business, and in the face of digital access to every book ever written, the shop prospered. Not a bad kind of treadmill, if she had to stick it out longer than expected.

A door slammed open down the hall, followed by thumping steps. Teagan, who couldn't leave or enter a room without banging a door, must have heard her thoughts, but it was her turn for a break. When she appeared in the doorway, hands on hips, Cait stood up and smiled.

"I guess I better get back in case book-starved customers are lining up."

"We'll hear the bell. I want to talk to you."

"Uh-oh, am I about to get fired?"

"Fired? No. I just want to make sure I understand why you want this job so, so, desperately, it seems. Or maybe not this job in particular but to work in a school? With snotty high school kids? I thought you had your fill of that when you did all those summer camp things. And a counsellor? I don't get it. You're not that much older than them. And no taller."

5: February: Visions

Cait smiled at Nathan. Easily this time. The question wasn't a surprise. When she had ventured into the halls, she had received inquiring looks. She had met each with eye-contact and a smiling nod, had straightened her spine, and walked with purpose on rubber knees. They were just kids for heaven's sake, not soul-eating zombies.

"I'm more than eight years older than you. I did a few years at university then changed my program and started over."

"Why?" Again, Nathan's voice held no challenge, just honest curiosity.

Cait gazed inwardly into the fading past of distant events. She hadn't shared with anybody what had happened to cause her to change programs, not even Teagan. Was that the right thing to do? What if one of her students were in the same situation? What would she tell them?

"You did great as an intern at the paper," Teagan had said. "They as good as offered you a job." Which was true.

She didn't tell Teagan about the smarmy creep who made the offer. Or about his other offer. She left her internship two days early and went back to campus.

Then she had the dream, or hallucination or whatever it was. She didn't tell anybody about that either. She just dropped journalism and registered in a different program.

"You're nuts!" Teagan had said. "You've worked so hard to get this far and now you're chucking it? For another four years, at least?"

Her parents were surprised. Mum opened her mouth, but then continued entering receipts into her computer. Dad, with his innate intuition, had only nodded and said she should go for it. But he had ditched pre-med to follow his dream of being a musician.

She unclasped her hands and breathed. Nathan seemed like a decent kid. He was interested and at least he was talking. She had read one thing in the file: Sam Goode had noted that he wouldn't 'engage in a meaningful discussion.' Should she share *the-thing-she-saw* with Nathan? Would he understand?

"It's kind of bizarre," Cait said, "but I was sitting on a bench on the quad between classes, and this scene formed in my mind: a student in a high school had a big problem and I had to help. The image just bloomed there and that's all I could see. Then I knew that's what I really wanted to do. Not just a teacher. I had to be a counsellor."

"A vision?"

"Yes. I suppose it was."

"Who was the student? Somebody you knew?"

"No…." The amorphous face hovered in the back of her mind.

"Did you have it just the once? Or did it come to you again? Later?"

Cait's stomach writhed. She shut her eyes. It had been a powerful revelation.

Sitting on that bench in the quad that day, she had had to bend over, and focus on the tiny weeds growing between the pavers. Throwing up would be so humiliating. Her head felt like it would float away. It took several minutes of deep breathing before she could get up.

It wasn't until she had enrolled in the new program, in a different university, that the visualization, or whatever it was, retreated from the forefront of her mind. Should she share that with Nathan?

"Why? Does this have anything to do with what you just told me?"

Nathan didn't smile. She had a feeling that smiling wasn't his usual expression, but his face softened, like a rock seen under water. "It might," he said. He lifted his shoulders and sat up. "But you probably won't believe me."

"What I believe doesn't matter. I can't help you if I don't understand what's bothering you."

6: February: Victim

Cait waited. Nathan looked over her head out the window. She bit the inside of her cheek. *Be patient. He will explain when he's ready. Or not.* Maybe there was nothing to explain, and he was taking advantage of his time with her to avoid English or Biology.

Nathan met her eyes and sighed.

"Do you think other people have visions like you did?"

"I don't know. I've never thought about it." Once she embarked on the new course, she didn't like to think about what had made her re-aim her career trajectory. Or what had made the decision for her. "Nathan, just tell me what this is about. Neither of us is getting any younger."

Nathan's cheek tic appeared and disappeared as quickly as the half-smile.

"Well you see, C– Miss Lee, like you, I see things that haven't happened yet. Or sometimes I have visions or dreams that come true. When I do, it always happens just like I see. I used to think it was fun. When I was ten, I told my mother her car would get smashed in the parking lot at her work. It did, but when I told her I had warned her, she shushed me up."

Cait stiffened but kept her grip on the chair arms relaxed.

"I've seen some other stuff. I used to think everybody could. Yesterday, I had a vision of Robbie Briggs at his locker moving his backpack out of the way to get his soccer shoes. Today he told me he couldn't find his phone, but I told him to go look in a shoe."

Cait resisted the urge to ask him if the phone was there. Whether it was or not didn't matter. What did matter was that Nathan believed he had foreseen it being there. Instead, she said, "But Nathan, those incidents could have been coincidences, easily explained."

Nathan looked down. Cait tensed. Was logic the wrong approach? Maybe she should have let him elaborate, give her more instances. Asked him questions rather than lecture about coincidences.

Nathan raised his head, "No..." He blinked. His gazed fixed and his eyes widened. He shuddered and swallowed. "Miss Lee, in fifteen seconds your phone will ring. It will be your new dentist confirming your appointment tomorrow. Then Mr. Kinney will come in here, excuse the interruption, and tell me that Miss Feenwell has dropped her complaint."

Before Cait could open her mouth, her phone rang, and she automatically answered her dentist's clerk. Before she finished stammering her thanks for the reminder, Art Kinney pushed her door open and strode inside.

Mr. Kinney nodded at Cait but hovered over Nathan. "Ah, excuse me, Miss Lee. Nathan. You're a lucky young man. Miss Feenwell has recovered from her shock. She must like you because she won't pursue her complaint. She thinks it was just bad timing for you." He nodded to Cait and marched to the door.

"Mr. Kinney," Cait said, her voice a trifle higher than she liked, "wait. There's something we should talk about. Nathan believes he sees things which can predict the future, but we were just beginning this discussion. Perhaps you should join us? He did say my phone would ring and that you would come in."

Cait looked at Nathan. Light flashed in his agate eyes. He shook his head, setting glossy hanks of hair in motion.

Cait paused, but the words spilled out. "And he has another worry which I believe is more important."

Mr. Kinney turned slowly from the door and stared at Nathan.

"More of your predictions, Nathan?" Then he turned to Cait. "Really Miss Lee, I think you are the victim of another of Nathan's little jokes."

"Joke? But, there's more to it…I think," Cait shivered. Nathan's predictions could be explained by observant guesswork, but why did he think he was going to die?

"Nathan, you're dismissed." Mr. Kinney pointed to the door. "Go back to your class." Nathan was already up and moving and left without a backward look.

"Mr. Kinney," Cait began.

"Miss Lee. Cait. I didn't expect you to buy into Nathan's fantasies. I did expect you to get him sorted out."

Sorted out? As if he were six and had lost his favourite crayon?

"You should have told him that throwing chairs and verbal attacks on unsuspecting people are childish behaviours and not acceptable. You should have at least got an apology out of him."

"Yes, I'm sure he's apologetic. He talked to Dave Grewal. He'll see Miss Feenwell too. But there is more going on. He told me he believes he is going to die."

Mr. Kinney had reached for the door, but stopped, frozen in place. "Die? As in commit suicide?" He stepped back, and in slow motion his brows rose, as did a hand, which he dropped before it reached his moustache.

Cait shook her head. "No, not suicide. I don't think so. We didn't get a chance to talk more about that."

Mr. Kinney's brows returned to normal, and he took a deep breath. "Did you read all of Nathan's file?"

"Well, no…," Cait said. "I started reading when you gave it to me, but then Nathan came to see me soon after."

"I see. When you get around to reading the whole of it, you'll find that some teachers have reported he often gazes into space or out the window when he should be taking notes or listening to instruction." Mr. Kinney rubbed his moustache and opened the door. "He has an active imagination and creates whole scenarios in his mind that he tells other students. He's also been treated for–"

"But I think he really believes he has visions that predict things…."

"Like your dentist calling? He could have read your silly little desk calendar." He pinched the bridge of his nose and closed his eyes. "And he could have seen me talking to Feenwell. You don't believe that Nathan can foretell the future, do you?"

Cait stared at her desk calendar. A big circle around tomorrow's date and 'DENT' above it. She saw Nathan rigid and glassy-eyed, and then her phone rang. And Mr. Kinney came through her door. But no use trying to convince him. He would say it was part of the act. Was it an act?

"He can't foretell his own death any more than you or me." Mr. Kinney glared at Cait. She felt the urge to step back. "Don't get me wrong, Cait. We can't dismiss this even if Nathan has disrupted the school with one of his predictions before–which you would know if you had read the file. Especially now he's mentioned this fear of dying. This is worrisome. He's obviously disturbed, and we can't take the chance he isn't having an episode of mental illness. I'll make time to report this to his parents." He clicked his tongue. "You take a breath and have a closer read of that file. You may take it home with you over the weekend."

7: January: Bookshop

Teagan locked the door and turned off the 'Open' sign. "What are you reading?"

Cait usually scrolled through her phone while Teagan went through the closing procedure, but the book she had taken from the shelf refused to leave her hands. Way better than cat videos, if the first few pages were a good indication.

"This." She held it up. On the front, a black crow flew across the yellow cover.

She had thought the story was about the crow, but no, it was about a woman with a brain tumour. Intriguing and possibly depressing. But she thought it would give her own brain a break. Lately, she had spent far too much time staring into screens of one kind or another until her entire skull ached. She couldn't stop job hunting yet. It was a lot of square-eyed work. Reading black words on a soft cream background was a relief. After the first few pages, the story had drawn her in.

"Yup, that's a good one. But kind of a sad…oops, never mind!"

R. Rigsby

"May I borrow it? Until tomorrow morning. I'll take care of it. Maybe write up a 'staff favourite' report for the website."

8: February: Dave

Cait leaned back in her chair with Nathan's file on her lap. She flipped a few pages and put a hand to her forehead as if it might help her concentrate. Maybe something to do with her warm cheeks and crushed ego. What a great start to her new job.

Her mind, with a mind of its own, flashed back to a few weeks ago when she drove Teagan's rattletrap truck home to tell her mother, and Firefly, about the job. Such high hopes. Such anticipation. Except for the creepy crow squawking at her.

So, now, not even a week in, and Mr. Kinney, who had usurped the responsibility to report to Nathan's parents, thought she was a gullible lightweight.

The lightweight expected Nathan's parents would talk to him over the weekend and take steps to intervene, if this was a plea for help, and not just another attention-grab as Mr. Kinney seemed to believe. She would see Nathan on Monday and ask if talking to his parents had helped. Assuming his parents understood the magnitude of the problem. They might not have been aware that Nathan was going through some kind of crisis. Which, come to think of it, he still hadn't explained. There was more going on with Nathan, of that she was certain. She hadn't heard everything yet.

She put the file in her bag. Reading would be easier at home, where it was quiet. She reviewed the school calendar. Pink Shirt Day was coming up. Everybody needed reinforcement of what was not just school policy, but a better social awareness. Bullies still needed redirection and those bullied needed protection. She would find out how this school supported that. Family Day and Spring Break coming up too. Would she go home for the break? Probably. She missed her horse. And she could share with Teagan her first twelve weeks on the job. If she lasted twelve weeks. Right now twelve days was looking iffy.

"Hi, got a minute?"

Cait jumped. Another tall person in her doorway, but not Nathan. Her eyes took a few seconds to refocus after staring into her computer screen. Dave Grewal. Mr. Kinney had introduced them on Monday morning, and she had spoken to him in passing, but hadn't yet had a one-on-one conversation with him.

"Oh, hi. Sure, come in." Shouldn't he be teaching? "Is there a problem in your class?"

"No, I've mastered the art of being in two places at once. Like in Harry Potter. Comes in handy around here." He grinned. "And I'm a mind reader. I've gotten good at that too. Even more useful than time-bending."

Cait laughed. "Every thought shows on my face."

"Be assured everything is fine. I have a student teacher who has taken charge of my gym class. Thought I would take the opportunity to say 'hello' properly and find out how things are going."

Cait replied that things were great, she was so glad to be here, loved the school, loved the town, but another part of her mind wondered. Was it coincidence that he chose today to delegate to the student after this business with Nathan? Had he talked to Mr. Kinney? Did he know about Nathan's revelations of the morning?

"Mr. Kinney said you had a chat with the boy called Nathan. You know I talked to him too," she said.

"I do."

"I can't share details, right?"

"I understand, but the tele-teacher-network is vibrating. But really, I came to see you because I'm worried about Nathan. I'm sure you are too, now that you've met him."

"I have concerns, yes. Have you talked with him often? More than Sam Goode, perhaps?"

Dave shrugged. "I only started here in September, but Nathan is in my home room and Math class. A smart kid. Often stays behind to ask questions, which often leads to general conversation. He's serious. Reserved. But has a quirky sense of humour, in his own way. I haven't seen much humour since November. He's been withdrawn. Morose even. Sam tried. It might have been easier if he'd turned up his hearing aids. Nathan said he got tired of yelling so loud that everybody in the hall could hear him."

"Have you met his parents?"

"No. They both work, and his father travels a lot."

"I know what that's like. My dad's a musician in a band. Back and forth across two countries and sometimes he goes to Europe. But when I was a kid, he called me every day from wherever he was."

"Nathan has never said anything about missing his dad. I don't think he's unhappy at home, but he might spend too much time alone."

Fantasizing? Making things up? Cait heard Mr. Kinney in her head. Maybe she had jumped the gun on this. Gullible? Or naïve? "Mr. Kinney said he would let the parents know what happened." Then she added quickly. "About the chair throwing and upsetting Miss Feenwell."

Dave cocked an eyebrow. "Just that?"

Cait set her chin.

"Never mind." Dave said. "I hope Nathan's parents find time to talk to him. He needs somebody to listen to him."

"Or he needs somebody to at least take him seriously. There are reasons for these outbursts."

The bell clanged in the hallway which filled with elated teens all bent on escaping for the weekend.

Dave grinned. "I better go see if my student teacher is hiding under the bleachers." He paused in the doorway and looked up and down the hall behind him. "I'm not sure that Kinney is seeing the big picture here." Then he was gone.

9: January: Kitchen I

Cait looked at the drying crusts of her lunch sandwich and blotted drips of tea with the paper towel she had used as a napkin. She pushed the phone out of auto-pilot reach. She would have to make a conscious effort to pick it up when the message came through. It had to. Her mind played a reel of herself dancing around in glee.

But waiting was so tedious. Not that there was a shortage of ways to fill her day. Teagan, in her capacity as hard-nosed entrepreneur, had lots of jobs that kept the bookshop in the black, apart from helping customers and shelving books. The afternoon task would be unshelving those to be returned to the publisher or had become spoiled from the grubby thumbs of too many non-buying readers. Like hers. But she had bought the book with the crow on the cover.

Teagan clomped up the stairs.

"You look hungry," Cait said.

"And you still look unemployed. Are you ever getting off my couch?"

"Hey, you were the one who offered it." Cait laughed and Teagan snorted.

"I know. And I know you can't get another place to live on the pitiful salary I pay you." But really, I'm surprised you've lasted this long sleeping on that lumpy couch. Talk about resolution. Those twits from the schoolboard would let you know if you didn't get the job, wouldn't they?"

"I'm hoping they'll let me know today. It's almost two weeks."

Cait drank the last of her tea and nibbled a crust. Working with Teagan wasn't so bad, despite the couch, and if there was one advantage with books, they didn't require feeding, like horses. Here, she could enjoy a guilt-free lunch. As Teagan was doing. The fridge opened and closed a dozen times, and a frying pan clanged onto the burner.

"Grilled cheese again?"

"Great guess."

Cait opened her book and read while Teagan burned her sandwich. When her phone pinged, she frowned from deep within her fictional world. Then surfaced with a start. One glance at the phone and she held her breath. It could be a courtesy call to tell her thanks, but no thanks. She would be shelving books forever.

Cait jigged around the kitchen; her phone held like a precious gift.

"So, good news I take it." Teagan lowered her sandwich.

"Yes, yes, yes! I got the job!" Cait stuck her phone in front of Teagan's face.

"You start week after next?" Teagan took the phone and squinted at the message. "Cait, this contract is for the balance of this school year–only about five months."

"I know."

"And it's not anywhere near here. It's, I don't know, at least half a day's drive from here. In the interior."

"It's only about eight hours driving." Cait repossessed her phone. "That's okay. And I don't mind the interior. I've done a lot of horse events there. Lovely in the summer."

"More like stinking hot. And a ton of snow in winter. Like now. And, really, Boondockville at any time. You like going to concerts and stuff."

"I'm sure it's not a cultural backwater. And it'll be a jumping off point. I'll keep my head down, do a good job, and keep applying for positions here."

"Sure." Teagan didn't sound at all sure. "But I have a bad feeling about this."

She sounded sure about that, but Cait was rereading the message and forming her reply. She would accept, with pleasure. Again that feeling of urgency. Was she just so done with the bookshop? With Teagan's fussing?

R. Rigsby

10: February: Pokey

Dave's words were still on Cait's mind even after she went home, nuked a couple of frozen burritos for dinner, and opened Nathan's file. She reread one comment, made a note, and read on. She was right when she had guessed he was a good student. Maybe even gifted. But not that kind of gift. His fear, or his belief he was going to die, was real, but please not because he believed he could predict a ringing phone. Come on. Or where a lost cell phone could be found.

Many people claimed to have visions that gave them clairvoyance and insight. Her vision wasn't a prediction. It merely showed her a possibility–one that had been in her subconscious all along. It could have been triggered by that unsavoury incident at her internship. She shuddered. She had made her own choice about switching programs. Nathan's visions were coincidences.

The next morning, Saturday, she went to her dental checkup. She had wondered if the annoying headache had something to do with clenching her jaw or grinding her teeth at night. Her new dentist said she rarely saw such good teeth with not a sign of unusual wear.

"Do you always call reminders?" Cait asked the desk clerk while pulling on her coat. Because he was simultaneously keying something into his computer and taking a call, he said something offhand about doing their best.

Cait then caught a bus that took her to within a kilometre of a riding stable outside of town. Sometimes it helped that her mother knew every such enterprise in the province. With recommendations. She tramped up the driveway, lugging her backpack, and kept to the packed tire tracks between the snowbanks. She was glad she hadn't brought Firefly up here after all. She wouldn't have the time for her, and her mother said that Firefly was getting lots of pats, extra carrots, and enough exercise.

Unlike her. This was the first day in over a week that she had walked more than a hundred meters at a stretch. A pounding ride would give her muscles a workout.

"I have Pokey ready for you," said a woman leading a bay gelding out of the barn. "He's a good guy, bomb-proof, and has great gaits."

Pokey? Maybe the ride wouldn't be the workout she had anticipated. Which was okay too. She could use some thinking time. And really, this wasn't home where she knew every trail and sideroad. Pokey lowered his head and swished his tail while she mounted and tightened her helmet. A slight squeeze of her legs and he moved off a at sedate walk.

The bridle paths were under a foot of snow, so, with the manager's directions, Cait and her mount headed to the cleared lanes and byways near the stable. So good to be again on a horse. Pokey too seemed happy to be out on a sunny, but cold day. His ears waggled and his head bobbed in unison when Cait urged him to a comfortable trot. She relaxed, trusting her unfamiliar mount, and let the therapy of horse and rider communion do its job.

What was it about Art Kinney? And him not getting the whole picture, like Dave said. Sure, he was older than her, and Dave. Probably at least as old as her parents. Parents who had never treated her as a child and had always spoken to her as an equal. Not that they didn't worry or fuss. Or offer opinions. Pokey's trot slowed to a walk as they traversed a slushy puddle on the side of the road. At least he had his mind on his job. Cait guided him past to the packed road, but her thoughts slipped back to her own job.

Art Kinney was about as patient with her as he was with any of the students, which wasn't much to say. Was that his problem? He couldn't see beyond her youth. Did he lump her in with the rest of the students who would be gone by the end of June. Like her?

His dismissiveness irked her, for sure. Five days with the man and she wanted to throttle him. So how would any student feel who hadn't the experience or confidence to stand up to such treatment? Was his lack of respect like bullying? Any reaction would be considered undisciplined or insolent. Any reaction on her part could get her fired.

Did that partly explain Nathan's outbursts? He seemed embarrassed by his loss of control. What had happened that had upset him so much? Whatever it was had been scary. Nightmares could be scary, and sometimes the fear remained after waking up. Whatever was troubling Nathan hadn't gone away. He had said he was going to die. No theatrics. Just a statement. He believed it.

Enough. She was here to enjoy being in a saddle again, the fresh crisp air, the brightness of the snow. She squinted her eyes against the glare. She knew something was wrong as soon as she saw the horse's ears pitch forward and felt his body tense.

She saw what would happen next. The vision flashed through her mind before Pokey hunched his back, leapt sideways, bucked, and whirled.

Despite the forewarning, her flight through the air came as a shock. Crows burst up from the side of the road, going up as she was coming down. She landed half in, half out of the snow-filled ditch with a good view of Pokey's rump heading for home. Beside her lay the remains of a furry carcass, identity impossible.

Cait stood up. Pokey was afraid of a few birds? Or was it the slight whiff of carrion? She brushed snow off her breeches and out of the neck of her jacket. When she plodded into the stable's yard, the manager held Pokey's reins, soothing the quivering horse. Apologetic, and dumbfounded, she declined payment. Cait said that because of the snow, she hadn't been hurt, just shaken up, and was fine.

It's not like she had never been dumped off a horse. She should pay more attention with a new horse. She grinned despite her irritation with herself. She knew better than that. Probably applied to a lot of things. The crows were a good reminder.

The stable manager gave her a lift home, still apologizing. Despite the upending, Cait slept well Saturday night and spent most of Sunday opening more boxes and putting things away in her apartment.

She had told Dave she liked her new place and that was true. It was small but all she needed. She had never lived alone before. After leaving home, she had either shared a dorm room or later an apartment. Always something going on in both places, not always helpful for studying or writing essays or clearing your head. This little space was a retreat after a long day.

Maybe next week the other teachers would be friendlier. But she was tired of being cut-off in mid-sentence. Jen was nice. She wasn't a teacher though. They probably all knew about Nathan's fear of death even though that should be confidential. Did they think she was an idiot for taking Nathan seriously? She would make sure Kinney understood that it wasn't Nathan's predictions she took seriously, but his fear. That was real.

R. Rigsby

11: February: Tracks

Her phone buzzed a warning, but Cait was already up and dressed on Monday morning. Despite the 'unscheduled dismount' from Pokey, Saturday's ride had worked its usual magic. Riding and thinking always helped clear her head, which now felt less cluttered than it had for weeks. She could deal with Mr. Kinney; she would find out what was upsetting Nathan. She would make a place for herself in this school.

What to do first today? If the blinking bus ever came. She shivered at the bus stop. Teagan was right. It was cold in this part of the province. She stamped her feet. Kinney first, then. Make him understand her concerns for Nathan. She didn't want to be shut out of helping Nathan, whatever form the process took. She was the counsellor.

In fact, she would talk to Nathan as soon as possible. They would explore his fears. He was complicated but they had made a connection. With her support, his parents' involvement, and the understanding of school staff, he need not battle this thing alone. If he needed professional help, she would guide him in that direction.

Her projected problem-solving continued on the bus-ride over the river where sheets of crumpled ice slid over the slow-moving water. She hadn't had time to visit any of the riverside parks to take in the extent of this impressive river. In the spring, its flow would increase in quantity and rate, going from winter somnolence to spring torrent. From benign to dangerous. That would be amazing to see.

She was early to the school, but a student climbed the front steps ahead of her. His toque hung out of one pocket, and he tossed his head as he hiked up the stairs. Black hair. Nathan. How perfectly timed.

"Nathan!" Cait stepped up behind him. Then she smiled. "Sorry, I should say 'good morning' before I launch into counsellor mode." And laughed.

Nathan grinned, the first she had seen. "That's okay, I'm not into student mode yet."

"Did you have a good weekend? Do anything fun?" What did kids his age do for fun around here? If they hadn't spent the weekend in serious conversation with their parents.

The grin dissolved into a half-smile, the sad half the gloomiest she had seen, but he said, "I caught up on some homework. Robbie and I went to the arcade, and we went to the rink to watch the Bridgemen practice."

"That explains the happy half of your smile, but I would like to continue the talk we had on Friday. Maybe then you can tell me about the other half."

Nathan looked away across the parking lot and the snow-covered playing field. "When?" he said.

"Which class isn't your favourite? Mr. Grewal's math this morning?" Would Nathan understand she was being funny?

He grinned. "No, I like math and D–, Mr. Grewal. But I think I would like to see you first thing."

First thing was before the bell, but Cait had stowed her coat and logged into her computer. Nathan shut the door and sat on the edge of his chair, one knee jigging up and down.

Cait again rolled her chair from behind the desk. "Nathan, I finally read your file this weekend. I didn't know you had a dream about a fire in the school."

"Oh, that. Yeah, I did."

"Tell me."

"That was last year. And it wasn't a dream. A vision. Like the other things I knew would happen."

"I see. Did you tell your parents? Or just friends?"

He wrinkled his brow and shrugged. "Dad's away a lot, and Mum just gets upset. Besides, most kids think it's a joke."

Like a rerun of a bad tv show, Cait saw herself sailing off Pokey. The crows taking flight and cawing in annoyance. That helpless feeling of being airborne and knowing, that unlike the crows, her landing wouldn't be a picture of control and elegance. She sat very still. Was that a vision? If it was, she could have used it a few seconds earlier and prevented an up close and personal view of a road-kill. Had she ever had other episodes of seeing something before it happened? She had once seen herself failing a science exam in, what, grade eight? And she had failed. Miserably. The only test she had ever failed, which is probably why it stuck in her mind. She had blamed a cold combined with a nasty bout of allergy reactions, but still…

"But it's not a joke, is it?" she said. Nathan, looking at his still jigging knee, hadn't noticed her delayed response. "You aren't making this up. What else do you see?"

Nathan put his long fingers over his eyes. "I see Dad putting my Xbox on the top shelf of his closet. I see my mother driving me to hockey practice, but we'll be late because of an accident or something on the bridge."

"But there's more. Please tell me why you think you are going to die, and how long this has been troubling you."

Nathan tensed, his hands pressing his eyes.

"It might be like what you saw. Your vision. What you saw is what happened, right? You dropped journalism because in your vision you were helping kids. Like me."

"Well yes. But I believe that changing programs was my choice." Was it, really? How would admitting she had a vision help Nathan? And how much was influenced by a truly offensive advance? "Other things happened to make me rethink journalism. Nathan, just tell me what you see. Then we can talk about why it is so upsetting."

"None of anything I've seen before is like what I'm seeing now–a bridge–it's not the car bridge, it's got tracks. The old rail trestle. Over and over. The same vision."

"What trestle?" An image of a dark bridge flashed across her mind. As if the bridge mattered. What mattered was Nathan's distress. "What do you see happening on the bridge?"

"First I see the tracks leading away into blackness. I follow them. Then I'm up high, looking down and hanging on. There's water below, moving fast and black. Then I'm falling. The bridge above is getting smaller as I fall. At least I'm sure it's me. I don't know if I fall or jump. There are angles all around." Nathan's hands slowly fell to his lap. He opened his eyes.

Cait let out a breath and croaked, "Why? Not why you're on a bridge. Why do you think you have this vision?"

"I don't know. Thinking about it makes me sick. And dizzy. It takes over my head again and again." Nathan leaned over his lap and rested his forehead on his fists. He lifted his head and stared at her. "This isn't anything like the other things I see." His lip trembled. Water rose in the stone-brown eyes. "I see it when I go to bed, I see it in my sleep, and I see it when I'm awake. I try to push it down and not let it take over my mind, but if I forget to concentrate on ignoring it, it springs out when I'm walking down the hall or opening my locker. I'm afraid to look in my lunch bag. I don't want to die. I don't want anybody to die."

Cait's mind felt like a washing machine. One that had started without a full load, but she disentangled the two things in her mind. Dreaming or envisioning an event was one thing, but the reasons it kept occurring might be something else. She stood up and walked to the window. She wished she wore glasses so she could take them off and wipe them. Her eyes ached. Was she getting the whole picture? She turned and leaned on her knuckles on her desk.

"I'm glad you shared this with me. I know it isn't easy for you. But we'll get it figured out, right? There's a reasonable explanation for these dreams. Visions. As horrible as they are, they aren't real, right?"

Nathan sighed. "I want to believe that. I want it to stop. But it's always there. Sometimes stronger, like last Friday morning, in home room. Mr. Grewal's equations. I saw the tracks on the blackboard. Then again at lunch. Miss Feenwell opened an oven to take out a pan of that gloop she makes."

The most tasteless mac and cheese ever. Cait blinked. Hard. But the image of the black depths of the oven with its steel racks persisted.

"You said May when we first spoke. How do you know the month? What makes you think that whatever you see will happen this coming May?"

"Oh. Because I see a calendar flicking—like that one." He pointed at the desk calendar. "It always ends at May. This year."

Cait's skin rippled under the sleeves of her cardigan. By the end of May, she could be looking at a few things coming to an end. So far, she hadn't done a fabulous job of keeping her head down. But the good thing was that May was over three months away. Time, then, was on their side.

"I will help you as best I can. We'll work on this. There must be a rational explanation. Did your parents talk to you this weekend?"

"Dad is in Vancouver. Mum had to work two shifts." He shrugged.

Cait forced her face to retain its professional smile. Really? Well, who can judge? "If you have this vision again, come and see me right away. Maybe if we talk about it while it's all fresh in your mind, it will help."

Nathan nodded and got up. A flicker crossed his face. "Yes. When it happens, I try to push it out of my head. It might be good to talk when it's still there. It's always there, I mean, before it makes me do something."

"Here's my number." Cait scribbled on a sticky note. "Call me if we're not in school. We can talk anytime."

Nathan's shoulders relaxed, and that tic of a smile formed in his cheek. He left.

Cait went to the window and tapped the window ledge. She needed time to think about this. But not too long. Her training had covered suicidal teens, but she hadn't expected to deal with an at-risk child so soon into the job. If Nathan *was* suicidal. He had never said that he would take his own life, just that he believed he would die. Before the end of May.

She had to report to Art Kinney about Nathan's horrible bridge vision. Should Nathan be there too? No. Art's bedside manner seemed a bit lacking, and Nathan needed understanding and support, not discipline and dismissiveness. She would like to update Nathan's parents too with the new information. Nathan wasn't likely suicidal, but the frightening visions of death must be addressed. Rather than showing up in his office like a truant, Cait called Jen. Would she ask Mr. Kinney for a moment? No? He wouldn't be in today. A meeting with the schoolboard.

She put down the phone. Tomorrow with Art then. In the meantime, Nathan would come to her if he needed help. They would work on this together, she had said. How exactly? She sighed. Nathan didn't wish harm to anybody, that was clear. As for predictions, they were probably just dreams, maybe he had many, but he only obsessed on the ones that came true. And maybe something in his psyche caused him to cling to the scary ones. A brief image of crows flew across her mind. No. Predictions seemed less likely as the day ticked by. How could it be true?

12: January: Kitchen II

Cait dropped her plate and glass into the sink. Good lunch and great news, but Teagan hadn't picked up her sandwich.

"Are you sure this is the job you want, Cait?"

"Of course it is."

Teagan smiled, but she wasn't done. "It seems rather rushed. Are counsellors that much in demand?"

"This school needs one. That's all I know. Why would I question that?" Did her voice show her irritation? Sometimes Teagan was more like her mother than her mother.

"It sounds like a big responsibility, Cait. Are you sure you're ready?"

"I guess I better be." She was certainly ready to meet new people who wouldn't coddle her as if she couldn't possibly manage her own life.

Teagan looked at Cait, then shrugged. "Will you call them to confirm? When you go downstairs. To work? Those books won't jump into the boxes themselves."

Cait laughed. Teagan meant well. Everybody meant well. From the landing she said, "Will do. And, T, can I borrow your pick-up when I'm done?"

"Sure. Where are you off to?"

"To tell Firefly. And I'll see Mum."

"That old horse gets to hear everything, doesn't she?" Teagan said. "Make sure you tell her you were picked out of dozens and dozens of applicants." Her barking laugh followed Cait downstairs.

Teagan was joking, but Cait shook her head. She had suppressed the niggling suspicion that they either hadn't had many applications or had had a lot. Maybe they got her mixed up with somebody else.

13: February: Dr. Brad

Black, black, black, pressed around her. Smothering, yet its formless void offered nothing to hold. Cait kicked and reached out–she was falling, plummeting into shapeless space. A flailing hand smacked the side of her nightstand. She woke with arms splayed, one hand throbbing. Ouch. Damn. That hurt. She blinked and rubbed her hand. Only a dream. But the falling sensation and vertigo lingered. Was she reliving Pokey's ejection and the snow-covered ground rushing up to her face? She lay still and practiced controlled breathing until the vertigo subsided. She hardly ever had bad dreams. And the vertigo, what was that about? The cheese omelette for dinner?

She fell into a sodden sleep and didn't hear her alarm, had no time to eat, and ran for her bus. When she pushed through her office door, Art Kinney stood, hands in pockets, looking out the window.

"Ah, Cait, here you are. Come to my office. We're meeting with Dr. Calder."

Why hadn't he emailed or messaged her? It wasn't yet eight. And who was Dr. Calder? Cait shook her coat off onto her chair, and in her boots, clumped behind Mr. Kinney to his office.

"This is Brad Calder," Art said.

Cait shook Dr. Calder's hand. About the same age as the principal, but a better smile.

Art Kinney bared his teeth, adding, "He's our medical liaison."

Medical liaison? This was the first she had heard there was such a person. But it was now only the second day of her second week, so maybe she would have met him, or been told of his existence eventually.

"I hear you met Nathan," Dr. Calder said. He glanced at Mr. Kinney, then cleared his throat. "Miss Lee, er, Cait, I'm sure you have learned that this is not the first time Nathan has made a prediction. Last year he said there would be a fire in the school on a certain Thursday morning."

Cait nodded. Yes, she had read that. And noted it. And asked Nathan about it, but there was nothing in the file about there being a fire. If there was a fire, did Nathan assume she knew about it? Should she have made more of it with him?

"Of course," he went on, "we spent a lot of time with Nathan then. His parents sent him to a psychiatrist and Sam Goode too saw Nathan often."

Sam Goode met Nathan often? Maybe he didn't think it necessary to make notations every time. Cait nodded as if in sage acknowledgement of her predecessor's dedication.

"Sam was a real pro. Shame about his ticker. Lousy Christmas gift," Art said, tapping his chest. He looked at Cait. "But he's recovering."

"I heard he fell while chasing a crow out of his garbage can…brought on the attack. I don't think he'll be …" Brad's voice trailed off. Cait looked from him to Art whose eyes fixed on Brad like one of those statues on Easter Island.

"We shall see," Art said. "Anyway, Sam followed up with everybody, saw Nathan almost daily, but Nathan kept insisting there would be a fire."

"Was there?" Cait said. "Nothing in the file mentioned that."

"No there wasn't. Not a real fire. In the cafeteria kitchen, during the lunch hour, Miss Feenwell accidentally left a greasy pan on the flame, and it did catch fire. She knew what to do though, smothered it with a lid, and turned off the gas. It caused a stir among the people in the cafeteria. Some of the kids ran forward all excited. They yelled and whipped out their phones. We had to open the fire doors and order everybody outside. A ridiculous commotion. Nathan had previously told anybody who would listen to him there would be a fire. But it was pure coincidence. Since then, no more predictions. Until now."

Art Kinney looked straight at Cait. "Are you sure you didn't say anything to him that encouraged him to tell you this latest death prediction nonsense?"

Cait stared. "No. Absolutely not!" Heat in her cheeks. The nerve of the man, to insinuate she was somehow responsible for what they clearly believed was one of Nathan's pranks.

She concentrated on what she hoped was a bland expression and said, "I'd never met him before yesterday, and, as you pointed out, I hadn't read his file. I had no idea he had predicted anything." Her knees trembled. How insubordinate was that? Did she want to be fired?

"Er, quite," Art said.

Cait held her breath for a full second and continued the effort to remain expressionless.

"Brad will advise Nathan's parents to send him to the same psychiatrist." Art said, while Brad examined his fingernails.

"Would the same psychiatrist not already have some pre-determined diagnosis?" Cait looked from one man to the other. "Are there any options for a different therapist? Shouldn't we talk about what we can do here to help Nathan? I know we can't share too much with his teachers, but they should know he may be vulnerable."

Cait waited, but both men had already risen. Cait stood up too, again looking from one to the other and waiting for a response, but the men moved to the door.

Dr. Calder turned his back to Cait and rested a hand on Kinney's shoulder. "Say, Art, do you think the Bridgemen will make it to the finals this year? I'm going to the game tonight. You?"

"You bet. Maybe see you in the concourse."

Both men chuckled, whatever had gone on between them earlier forgotten. Art fished in his pocket. Without looking at her, he handed Cait a bent and coffee-stained card.

"Here's the number for Nathan's shrink. Dr. Benjamin. Keep in touch with him, not that he's likely to give up much info–patient confidentiality and all that– we just need assurance that Nathan isn't a danger to himself or others. We don't want anything happening in the school."

The men walked away leaving Cait standing with the grubby card clutched in her fingers.

14: February: Death Wish

Cait kicked her boots off in her office, pulled her shoes out of her bag, and stomped into them. Locking her office behind her, she dodged students in the hallway. They knew who she was now, and they gave way as if pulsed aside by her outrage. She found Dave Grewal in the staffroom at his locker.

"Can you send Nathan to see me when he comes in?"

"Well good morning to you too."

Cait laughed. "Yes, sorry, good morning. Mine started off great, as you can probably tell."

"Oh, let me guess. You met Brad Calder." At her expression, he continued, "Met him on the stairs."

"We had a strained meeting. About Nathan. Calder is probably a good doctor, and it makes sense to have a medical liaison for the school. But it would have been good to know about him earlier."

"Yeah, I think he means well, but he leaves it up to Kinney to make decisions. I think he's still trying to get into Kinney's golf club."

"I'm not certain Mr. Kinney has Nathan's best interests in this. He's treating him as if he's an inconvenience. One that shouldn't mess up anything during school hours or cause the school embarrassment. Even if Nathan is acting something out, there are reasons for him doing so."

Three other teachers came in exchanging the usual morning moanings and eyed her and Dave, two with grins.

"No worries, I'll send that student to you as soon as I see him," Dave said.

"Thanks," Cait said. She nodded to the others and left. In her office, she looked up from locking her bag in the drawer and pulling out Nathan's file. A figure stood in the doorway, a murky silhouette against the fluorescent lights of the hall. Déjà vu. Nathan. And here so fast. She hadn't thought through everything she wanted to say to him, but she adjusted her counsellor smile as she invited him to shut the door and take a seat.

"Did you talk to your parents last night? Do they know about this terrible vision you keep having?"

"No. I don't want to talk to them. I can't. I've only told you." Nathan sat up and gripped the arms of the chair. "I don't want anybody else to know. Not even D– Mr. Grewal."

"I'm sorry Nathan, but Mr. Kinney has called in Dr. Calder."

"Kinney! And now Calder!" Nathan sprang to his feet. The chair tipped backwards–the thump on the carpet punctuated his shouted, "I thought this was just between us. I thought you were going to help me! I thought just you and me would talk this, this morning. You said I could call you anytime."

Cait stood up too. "You can call me, Nathan, and I will help you, as much as I am able. Dr. Calder will speak to your parents and recommend that you again see," she glanced at the card, "this Dr. Benjamin."

"He's a quack! He thinks I'm a spoiled only child with 'an active imagination.'"

Cait stepped back from Nathan's sneer and clenched fists. An invisible chasm widened between them.

"But I can't keep it between us now. I couldn't from the beginning. Not when you talked about dying. Mr. Kinney is doing what is right. You do understand, don't you?" That sounded so textbook. What could she say to bring him back?

"No! You could have kept quiet. I never want to talk to you again. And I do see things. All the time. Nobody believes me!"

Nathan swayed and then gripped the back of the chair, his eyes again fixed and as inanimate as marbles.

"A bird, a crow. It will smack into that window!"

Cait spun around and gasped. The glass vibrated with a ringing thud from the impact of a feathered body. She leaped to the window and spotted the dying crow, neck broken, beak opening and shutting in a puddle of dirty snow-water below.

She whirled around. One hand gripped the window ledge and the other reached for the back of her chair.

Blood pounded in her ears and her stomach heaved in warning. "Nathan! Did you see that coming?"

Nathan bent over the chair, his face white. "Noooo, not the real bird, but I saw it in my mind."

Cait had to sit down, but Nathan pushed himself upright.

"You probably don't believe that either."

Cait knew her face showed her shock, her disbelief, her, what, horror?

Nathan shrunk into himself, shoulders slumping. He let go of the chair and turned away. "I suppose you'll tell everybody about that too."

When the final bell echoed in the hall, Cait only heard the echoes of her door slamming when Nathan left. Long after the trample of student footsteps had subsided and classroom doors clicked shut, Cait leaned on her elbows at her desk. Nathan's open folder again sat in front of her. She stared into the pages, the card on top. Helpless to stop a tear sliding down her cheek, she recalled Nathan re-opening the door and his last words, in a resigned monotone, "I'm sorry."

Cait shook her head and swiped her tears. Sorry? For sharing his terror? For taking up her valuable time? For making up the whole thing? Except crows didn't commit suicide on the whims of overwrought teenagers.

15: April: Arcade

Months passed. Cait spoke to Nathan in several follow-up sessions. He didn't refuse to see her but only made glancing eye-contact. He answered all questions with monosyllabic replies. If he spoke at all. When she mentioned his visions, he just shook his head and looked farther away. What did he see?

The last time they met, Cait had again brought up the bridge and the tracks and asked if he still had the dreams. He had stared at the plant on her filing cabinet and asked her if she still had her vision. She had had to answer that this conversation was about him, not her. Straight from the textbook, but the Nathan she first met, cautious but hopeful, became smaller and more distant even though his physical presence remained sprawled in her guest chair.

Maybe this is what Sam Goode meant. Poor Mr. Goode. He'd suffered another attack in February, but Art Kinney said that Sam had bounced back better than his doctors expected. Cait wanted to ask if he planned to come back but hadn't had the heart. Maybe Sam wasn't as inept as she believed. Maybe she was inept. What could she do to bridge that distance with Nathan? None of the books told her that. None of them had any student-counsellor scenarios relating to Nathan's predicament. But she had had some positive bridge-building with other students, with good outcomes.

That girl who had her cell phone taken away seemed to get it when Cait said that, even if there wasn't a rule against cell phone use in class, it just didn't make sense to text the friend sitting next to her. Next time, she should pass a note. That was silly, they both knew it, but it was funny, and the girl laughed. She got the point.

Yet, when Cait passed Nathan in the hall, he looked right through her. Not a glimmer in his eyes, no hesitancy in stride, nothing to show that he saw her. She called Nathan's mother, but she said that there was no need to meet as she was confident that the psychiatrist was helping Nathan as he had before. Cait hoped that was true. His teachers said he no longer missed classes and was again completing assignments and participating in discussions.

Perhaps the doctor had reached Nathan, won his confidence, sorted out the meanings of his dreams, and helped him find peace of mind. Did Nathan tell the doctor about the crow? The image of exploding feathers, and the shock, had faded somewhat. Had it really happened the way she remembered? How could Nathan have guessed that would happen?

In late April, instead of catching her bus at the usual stop, Cait walked farther into town thinking that a walk on a sunny evening would help clear her mind.

Caitlyn Mai Lee, you have been a mole ignoring a beautiful spring. Much like you've been ignoring the headaches. Too much screen time and not enough fresh air.

She hadn't gone back to the stable. Nathan had been the first in a daily influx of students with problems and questions ranging from what classes they needed for university entrance to her ideas on acne treatments. She often researched at home on weekends to check college programs, and yes, acne treatments, despite referring such questions to the school nurse or Dr. Calder. She cited her busy schedule when the stable manager called asking if she would like to book a horse. A different horse.

She might go to the stable. It was high time to get outside and see something other than four walls and her computer screen. Maybe check out the yoga place on the next block. They did classes in the park in the summer.

The yoga studio was on the second floor above an arcade, but she couldn't find the stairs. She pushed through the arcade door thinking she could ask whoever ran the place.

It was like stepping into a cavern of whizzing laser beams with sound effects. Pops, bangs, whirs, and whines. The place even smelled of exhaust, hot rubber, and gunpowder. Normally, she loved arcades, but the flashing lights and thundering sound effects hurt everything behind her eyes. She put her hands to the sides of her head. This was new. She stood blinking, not seeing anybody who might qualify as a managerial presence, but she saw Nathan.

Almost engulfed by an immense machine, he stared into the depths of the curved screen. As usual, his hair hung over his forehead and flipped from side to side as one hand wrenched a control back and forth and the fingers of the other drummed a deathly tattoo on a panel of buttons. Something in his screen exploded and a humanistic figure fell shrieking into a boiling chasm.

Cait shuddered, and still not seeing anybody else, backed toward the door. Outside, she walked blindly a few steps almost tripping over the sidewalk sign indicating 'Yoga Upstairs.' Not caring about yoga, or the stairway she had missed, Cait tottered toward her bus stop. What was it about the arcade or Nathan's game that had her brain trying to burst her skull?

16: May: Nightmare

Cait thrashed and screamed. She sat up, heart pounding. No recollection of the nightmare, just a haze of sooty shapes against a smoke-yellow sky. She sipped some water. Early, early on a May morning. Not even light yet. Another bad dream. Maybe she should see a doctor.

She rolled over to sleep but didn't sleep. Instead, she saw herself and Nathan. They stood on a black brink, the hollowness of boundless space roaring in her ears. Shadowy beams angled left and right, their outlines fuzzy and black on black–where? A bridge? Like the train trestle? She begged Nathan to stop, stop…stop what? Then a strange beating noise, like a shaken paper bag. She sat up shaking and sweating. This one was no dream. Nathan was in trouble.

She grabbed her phone and stared at it. Nathan had her number, but she had no way to contact him. Art Kinney wouldn't be in his office so early, so she called his cell. No answer, just a prim invitation to leave a message. She didn't.

Dressing and calling a cab, she panted over the seat urging the disbelieving driver to "Hurry, hurry!" At the school, she pounded on the doors until the grumbling custodian let her in. In her office, she logged into her computer. Come on, come on. The slowest system in the free world. She pulled up Nathan's contact info and called the home number. A not-in-service message. What? She phoned his mother's cell, but it went to voicemail. A slight tremor in her voice as she left a message. Brad Calder's voicemail said he was on vacation, and the office number on the psychiatrist's card rang through to a recording advising that office hours began at nine.

Cait dashed down the hall to Nathan's home room. A few kids had arrived, including Robbie Briggs and the boy she knew as Ravi. Dave Grewal, a habitual early bird, wrote at the blackboard. He greeted her puffing inquiry about Nathan with a sideways look at the boys.

"What's the trouble?" He resumed writing on the blackboard, and answered with a low chuckle, as if they were discussing something of minor importance.

It wouldn't have mattered because the boys at the other end of the room were engrossed in their own discussion. Their low-pitched voices couldn't disguise the snarling exchange. Dave glanced at the boys and then at Cait.

"I don't know, exactly. Just a feeling. Something's not right."

"Just a feeling? Is there anything else?"

"Maybe." Cait tilted her head and closed her eyes, but Dave didn't press.

"If Nathan doesn't show right at nine, I'll let you know," he said. "Check with Jen. Maybe his mother has called. But tell me how this goes, will you?"

In the office, Jen, between answering a phone call and turning on her computer, told Cait that Nathan's mother hadn't called, but his father had. Nathan was unwell earlier and would be a few minutes late. He and his mother had just left home.

Cait felt herself deflating. All that overblown hype for nothing. What was wrong with her?

"Are you okay?" Jen took off her coat and folded it over an arm. "Did your life flash before your eyes?"

Cait breathed out slowly. She was an idiot. It was just a dream. A very vivid dream. Not a vision. How could she explain that to Jen?

"I'm fine. Thanks." She shrugged. "I may have over-reacted, but it's okay."

"That's what makes you so good at what you do."

Cait smoothed her hair and went into the staff washroom. She washed her face. In the mirror, her own brown eyes under her dark bangs reminded her of those stones she had seen in Nathan's face. Who was fine. He was with his mother. But maybe, she should make sure he was okay. Was he really sick, or had something else happened? The five-minute warning bell rang. Cait jumped.

She went back to the school office. She bit her lip as she poked her head into Mr. Kinney's office. Should she tell Art about her dream? No, she wouldn't mention the dream. She would say that she was again concerned about Nathan's state of mind. Based on what? Something would come to her.

"He's not there," Jen called. "Just came in and went right down to Dave Grewal's room. Some kind of fight. Probably over a girl."

Cait dropped her hands to her sides.

Nathan was with his mother and on his way here. Best not to talk to Kinney about her worries. Because of a dream. And it was a dream.

Cait walked to her office. Would the day hold some tearful confessions from a distraught girl who had no idea that flirting with boys could cause such a commotion?

Within minutes, Robbie Briggs stood in front of her desk with a split lip, blood on his shirt, and a scribbled note from Art Kinney. Any confessions wouldn't be from a girl.

"Robbie," she began in her best counsellor I-know-what-I'm-doing voice, "I understand you punched Ravi." She glanced at the wrinkled note, "Without provocation, according to Mr. Kinney. May I hear your side?"

"That ass–, er, jerk just said something about Nathan, that's all."

The hair on Cait's arms stood on end. Maybe she should have stuck with journalism, despite what had happened with her internship. When she went home on spring break, Teagan had sorted her out on a few things.

17: March: Spring Break

Cait stifled a sneeze into the corner of her elbow. The book she was shelving thumped to the floor. Another sneeze threatened as she leaned down to pick up the book. She had offered Teagan an afternoon of free labour.

"Is it the dust in here?" Teagan called from the desk where she was balancing the day's take.

"No. Delayed reaction. I helped Mum feed horses this morning."

"Speaking of delayed reactions, isn't it time you told me what really happened at the newspaper? And you haven't said much about the new job."

Cait stretched the kink out of her back and slid the book into place. Teagan would no doubt repay her confidence and free labour with unsolicited advice. But maybe she could use some advice about now. "Is the door locked?"

"That good, is it? Yeah, door's locked."

Cait told Teagan about the insinuating offer from her internship supervisor.

"You should have told his boss, Cait. The creep."

"Yes, but he didn't actually do anything except talk. And put his arm around my shoulders. He had awful breath."

"Didn't do anything? Like that doesn't count? You should have told me. I know people who deal with situations like this. He wouldn't have got away with it. What's more, he wouldn't be free to try it on with somebody else."

"I know. It isn't just about me, is it? That's why I called Professor King. Told her not to place anybody else there. And why. Maybe there are others who haven't said anything."

Teagan put her hands on her hips and screwed up her face. "So, are you getting the same kind of flak now? I understand you can't talk about this Nathan kid more than you already have, but is there something else going on?"

"There is friction, yes, between me and the principal, but not like that. I wasn't his first choice of replacement for poor Mr. Goode. I'm sure he won't want to renew my contract for September, but that's okay. I want a job in this city anyway."

Should she have let that one bad experience during her internship stall her first plan? Her mother had said that if the new program she had chosen didn't work out, she still had options, one of them being to take over the stable business. Her father, home from his band's tour, though, disagreed.

"Follow through, Cait, if that's what you want to do. Wasn't that your vision?" he had said, not realizing that her change in career flightpath had, in fact, been due to a vision.

Yes, the vision. Was it really as compelling as she remembered? Or did she use it an excuse not to face her cowardice in dealing with Mr. Creepo? Were visions real? Could they really predict the future? Or just influence choices? Black wings brushed her mind. The goosebumps on her arm raised higher, and unease tightened her innards.

"What else?" Teagan put the debit/credit machine in a drawer and dusted the counter with her sleeve.

"I don't know. Just a spooky feeling. Nathan is complicated. And I might be wrong about something."

18: May: Confessions

Robbie stared at her, his head tilted, his expression a quizzical frown. Cait subdued her anxiety and pushed her face into a professional smile. Then she dropped all pretense of cool professionalism. She leaned forward and looked Robbie right in the eyes. She was going to burn that textbook.

"You need to be honest with me. Forget that I'm a counsellor. Let's get this out in the open. What did Ravi say?"

Robbie glanced away, then inhaled. "He said Nathan is a freaking weirdo, and I am too for hanging around with him. That's it." He narrowed his eyes and thrust out his chin. "That's all."

"Nice try. I know there's more."

Robbie pulled back, but then blinked and looked at his barked knuckles.

"Come on, Robbie."

"Ravi said nobody should listen to a word Nathan says. Not that he's saying much these days."

"Robbie, you're worried about Nathan. I am too, and maybe you can help me help him."

"But Nathan is just home with the pukes, right? He's okay. I just talked to him."

Cait smiled. "You're a good friend for worrying. But I know he once told you where to find your cell phone. And maybe he's shared other things?"

Robbie's eyes went round. He jerked as if jabbed with a fork.

"But we both know he can't predict anything," Cait said, concentrating on keeping her voice low and calm. "He must have seen the phone drop in your shoe before but didn't tell you." Then, with a burst of forewarning, she asked, "What else did Ravi say?"

"He's always telling Nathan to go jump off a bridge. He thinks it's funny. This morning he asked me if Nathan had jumped. I told him to knock it off. He said he wouldn't be surprised if Nathan tried to fly off the bridge and I followed him. Like a lemming. Then I punched him."

Cait couldn't help the quick intake of breath. Was that it then? Nathan had this dream or vision or whatever it was because Ravi kept telling him to jump off a bridge? Something that any bully might say to a vulnerable kid? Were Nathan's dreams all related to repeated bullying? Was Robbie agitated because of the bullying or because Nathan had told him about the vision?

Before she could ask Robbie anything further, the bell rang and at the same time her computer pinged an alert to an email. She glanced at the screen. Robbie bolted.

Cait opened her mouth and raised her hand, but Robbie was gone. Sighing, she turned to read Jen's email. The message said that Nathan's mother had called. Nathan had vomited on the drive to school. They were back at home. Cait sat down, chin in hand. Her own dream swept through her mind again. Her head throbbed.

Just a stupid dream. She needed to get a grip.

19: May: Chemistry

Cait needed time to think about what Robbie had said. Perhaps Nathan was sharing more with Robbie than he was with his doctor. For now, he was safe at home. Her phone rang and her computer chimed another email alert at the same time a shy girl tapped on her door. Her next appointment.

Cait concentrated on giving the girl, who was freaking out, in her words, about final exams, her full attention. After a few minutes, they narrowed down her main concern to the Literature exam, for which there would certainly be an essay. Cait recommended that she review the books covered in the course, write a short paragraph about each, and check with the teacher to see if he had any other tips. She told the girl that the teachers were there to help, not merely critique her work. And to see her again if she still felt worried.

She called parents to discuss their children's academic plans for September and met with the district's school nurse about an upcoming video on venereal diseases. She referred a struggling student to a tutor, hoping last minute remedial action might salvage his year.

Later, she thought about Ravi and Nathan. Tormentors could be sneaky and say or do things which on the surface didn't look like bullying. Within seconds she knocked on Art Kinney's door. She walked in without waiting for the customary sideways glance and furrowed brows as a sign of invitation.

"Art," she said, and gave him the summarised version of her discussion with Robbie. "We need to do another round of reminders to reinforce the non-bullying policy–perhaps a 'Pink Shirt Day Spring Version,' with an assembly and a few student speakers. In fact, hand it off to the student council and let them have a go at it."

"Oh, that's probably not necessary. I think that day in February was sufficient." Something of her thoughts must have shown on Cait's face. "But I could do an address–"

"No. I think it would be more effective if the kids did it themselves. And more meaningful. In fact, I'm going to have a long talk with Ravi and ask him to participate in organizing the speeches. Along with Robbie."

"Is that wise? Both are trouble-makers if you ask me."

Cait refrained from saying that she wasn't asking him but decided to deflect the conversation to her other reason for pestering the pompous egotist masquerading as a poor overworked principal. She mentally bit her tongue. These were not good thoughts if she wanted a decent reference.

"Now about Nathan. As you rightfully mentioned months ago, his psychiatrist can't share anything with me. Yet, we need to understand Nathan's progress, so it might be time to have an informal meeting with his parents. They should know that his teachers, under your guidance, continue to monitor him. I'm sure they would talk to you."

"Yes, yes, an excellent thought, very good," Art said, "I'll call his parents today. I wish Sam were here. He was very good at this. Not that you aren't, of course, but he does have the advantage of age and experience, and he worked so well with Nathan."

Cait made her mouth form a smile. "I totally understand. I have learned so much from reading his notes."

Thanking him so much for his help, Cait pulled his office door shut with a little wave. Jen raised her eyebrows to which Cait grinned and winked. She was so bad.

Art called her a few minutes later about his chat with Nathan's parents. Then it was lunch hour, and she needed to walk off her agitation. And think. She was halfway down the steps when the door squeaked open behind her.

"Cait, may I join you?" Dave Grewal, shrugging into his jacket, let the door bang behind him.

"Oh, yes, of course," Cait said. "I usually do a few laps around the track." They crossed the parking lot, Dave's long strides keeping up with her efficient steps. "I'm sorry about this morning and my outburst about Nathan. It must have looked like borderline hysteria."

Dave grinned and shrugged. "It did surprise me. You always seem so composed and in control."

"Do I? Maybe it's just Nathan then. He's okay, by the way. I was going to tell you after my walk."

"Even after years of teaching, some kids still surprise me. Nathan has his issues, but he's a good kid."

"I think so too, but I haven't been able to talk to him for months. He's shut me out. Art spoke to his parents who are confident he's doing okay. Nobody has said anything more about his dreams, or visions, or predictions, or whatever they are...." Drat. She bit her lip. "Forget what I just said, okay." She stopped and looked up at Dave.

"It's fine. I had an idea of what was going on. Soon after I started here, some of the gossips were rehashing Nathan's history and brought up the fire prediction. So I asked him one afternoon after class. I could tell he was thinking about whether he should tell me, but I just went back to marking a math exercise. He only said that he sees things sometimes, but it was silly stuff and nobody was ever hurt. That was before he began to withdraw, and I wondered what had happened. But he never stuck around after class. There was more gossip about Nathan after he threw a chair at my blackboard and yelled at Miss Feenwell–"

"It wasn't Miss Feenwell. It was her oven."

"Yes, Nathan said so when he came to apologise, and we had another talk about the fire thing. I think he wanted to say more, but Kinney butted in and sent him to see you."

"Art seems to think that Sam Goode was able to get through to Nathan."

Dave snorted, then looked around. Nobody near them and only the track team practicing across the oval. "Listen, Cait. Sam wasn't the heroic saviour Art likes to portray. He's a nice guy and a decent counsellor but should have retired at least two years ago."

"I've guessed as much." Cait stopped and looked up at Dave. Funny, she hadn't really looked at him before. She had thought he was much older than her, as she did of all the other teachers, but he was probably only a few years older. But Sam Goode was old. Older. Did it really matter how old a person was if they were good at what they did? And were in tune with the people they worked with? From some odd or unrelated notations in students' files, she had concluded that Sam had mixed up some of the students.

Dave had stopped too and stood staring down at her.

Cait smiled. "I'm sad about Sam. His age shouldn't be a factor in determining competence, but neither should Nathan's. Just because he's young, doesn't mean he shouldn't be taken seriously. Not dismissed as a problem child trying to get attention. He believes his dreams or visions, so rather than trying to tell him that what he believes isn't possible, I hope the doctor is focussing on *why* he believes they are possible."

Dave nodded and looked toward the school where students and teachers were going back inside. "Do you think his visions are real? You had something like that yourself this morning, didn't you?"

Cait stopped walking. He didn't have a high opinion of Art Kinney's ability to imagine that there might be more to Nathan's dreams than just an excuse to get attention.

"I don't know what I had." Cait looked around at the brown track, the green spring grass, and trees finally leafed out. So serene and normal. Unlike her mind.

"But it worried you enough to come in early and try to find out."

The vision came back in all its clarity despite her best efforts all morning to forget it. And her last meetings with Nathan when he would still talk to her. She had tried to submerge that too. Trust Dave? "Do you know how this business with Nathan started? His 'predictions' about Art coming into my office and Miss Feenwell dropping her complaint?"

Dave smiled. "Remember that tele-teacher thing?"

"Did it include the bit about my dentist calling?"

"Nope, didn't get that." Dave frowned. She could almost see internal antennae waving.

He shook his head and Cait told him. "Art dismissed that too. He blamed it on Mr. Goode's desk calendar."

"It's uncanny, yes, but most of his so-called predictions could be just really good guesses or observant speculation," Dave said.

"I thought so too. When I had to tell Nathan about the Kinney & Calder tag team involving his psychiatrist, he was angry with me, and still is. I think his rage is a combination of his fear and his feeling of betrayal and helplessness. I tried to talk to him about it when we last met, but like the other times, no progress. I've lost his trust."

Dave nodded, listening, his eyes on her face. "He's always been a study of contradictions. On one hand, he shares some of his predictions, but the one big one, that really scares him, he keeps close. Like he's afraid that if he tells, it'll make it happen. Make it real. Yes, I know about his awful bridge dream."

"You do? When did he tell you?"

"A few weeks ago. After school. I gave him a lift downtown to see his doctor. I was being conversational when I asked him how it was going. Didn't expect an answer, but he said that he was going to tell the doctor about the vision. When I said 'what vision?' he told me. Positively chilling."

"It is." Cait hunched her shoulders in her coat. Brrr, she felt that chill, but such a relief that Nathan had reached out to Dave.

"Still, his vision isn't a prediction. He can't do that," Dave said.

"I've been telling myself so. It's not logical."

"But?"

"You don't know about the bird hitting my window, do you?"

Cait filled him in on Nathan's trance-like rigidity, how his voiced rasped a warning, and how she turned in time to see the crow, beak open, smashing into the glass, then how it so slowly fell away, its blood-filled beak broken, its feathers drifting where it died in the ice-rimmed puddle. She didn't tell him how she had tried to submerge that memory to some part of her mind that didn't like irrational, eerie, cue the do-do-do music here, encounters.

The bell rang. Dave stood until she took his sleeve and he, unspeaking, followed her to the doors.

20: May: The Trestle

The afternoon became a merry-go-round of people arriving and leaving Cait's office. Instead of horses or swans or pink pigs, students with questions, crises, or notes rotated through her guest chair.

She was too busy to turn and look out her window where she only saw birds with terror on their faces. She asked the last visitor to please leave her door open. Was the incipient claustrophobia due to the overwarm air in her office? She took a breath and opened the window. No birds of any kind out there, just the playing field, so green now, and such blue sky. She swore it was bluer than at home on the coast. The scents of May mingled with those of floor polish and locker contents.

Just after their lunchtime revelations, she had heard Dave haranguing a boy about the mess in his locker. It smelled like a compost heap. Throw out the old lunches, already. She had never heard him raise his voice before.

She stepped away from the window, closed the door, and made more phone calls, mostly to parents whose kids had skipped classes, hadn't provided notes, or had earned detentions. She wished more calls were to relay good news–a particularly insightful class discussion, a helpful hand to another student, anything positive.

She would ask the rest of the staff to let her know of any student's good-news actions. Some would be onboard, like Dave, and others. She now shared conversation and jokes with most teachers. When did that happen? They were a lot friendlier and those who remained aloof let her finish her sentences.

She updated her computer calendar and threw the paper desk calendar in the recycling bin. Poor Mr. Goode. A heart attack after chasing a crow. So sad, but the desk calendar had to go. Why hadn't she chucked it sooner? This was her office. Her desk.

Just after five, she logged off and took her bag out of the drawer. Out on the street waiting for her bus, she breathed slowly. Purposefully.

The day had ended well despite the frazzled start. And she was glad Nathan had shared his vision with Dave. Maybe the more he shared, the more opportunities for help and intervention would arise. Did he need intervention?

Should she have told Dave about the bird? It was part of a confidential conversation, but at least it explained her indecision over Nathan's dreams or visions. It didn't explain her own dreams. One minute she believed that Nathan could predict the future, and the next she dismissed it as teenage over-anxiety. But would Dave think she was losing it if he thought she believed the bird prediction? He hadn't said a word about whether he believed it or not.

Otherwise, everything else was going well. The kids greeted her in the hall with cheerful, but respectful 'hellos,' and she had overheard that she was easy to talk to. Maybe she was beginning to hit her stride and this thing with Nathan had been the first test. An ongoing test, yet to be resolved.

Cait watched the bus signalling for her stop. Could she patch things up with Nathan? She had told him in every meeting that even though he chose not to talk to her about his visions, she would always listen if he changed his mind. He remained mute on that subject. She would ask him to see her again. She hadn't apologized for involving Mr. Kinney, not that she had had a choice, but she was sorry. She would ask how he felt about his therapy. Maybe it was better this time. The last time they met, he had asked her about college programs. Was it a sign that he was no longer convinced he was going to die?

Beside the bus shelter, a crow pulled a crumpled wrapper out of the rubbish bin. It stopped and cocked its head at her, one glass-bead eye reflecting light. Cait looked away, stepped up onto the bus, and dropped into an empty seat. What luck. She relaxed, ready to enjoy the ride and the views. The image of the crow on the bin flashed through her mind. Nathan. Never far from her thoughts.

What a day. It felt like years since she woke, heart pounding and chest thumping with terror. She now understood Nathan's fear, especially if the vision overwhelmed his mind without warning. Her own dream had been terrifying, but it was just a nightmare. It meant nothing. It hovered in the back of her mind, but she could firmly shove it into the depths.

She would tell Nathan about it. It might be a way to reach him. Tomorrow then. She wouldn't give up. She swayed with the bus's movement and looked through the window, a hopeful smile showing in her pale reflection.

What bridge or trestle had figured in her dream, or in Nathan's dream? This city straddling the river was full of them. Her bus rumbled across a long span over that river, and below she could see the train bridge that had been there for years. Black creosote coated the struts and timbers. A crow winged across her line of vision.

Then she saw Nathan. Standing on the bridge. Looking up at the crow.

"No!" Cait screamed. She jumped up and pounded on the window. "Nathan, look at me, don't do it!" Trampling the toes of her startled seatmate, she shoved fellow passengers out of her way as she scrabbled to the door and grabbed the handles, all the while shouting, "There's a boy on the bridge, stop, stop–"

She pressed her face into the glass in the door. The bus had moved well past the point she had seen Nathan even as the driver hit the brakes and yelled at her to get away from the door. The bus jolted to a halt, she lost her footing and whirled backwards. Her feet skidded out and her head clunked the handrail.

Cait swam up to consciousness. Blood trickled down the side of her head. What seemed like a hundred open-mouthed faces gawped down at her. She elbowed herself up; lights flashed behind her eyes.

"The boy on the bridge! The boy on the bridge, stop him!"

The bus driver helped her to sit, and while restraining her from scrambling to her feet, he listened to her garbled story of seeing a boy on the train bridge who might have jumped. He relayed this to somebody on the other end of his phone.

"Yeah, yeah, that's what the lady says… Ma'am, they want to know…"

Cait slipped over the edge of a pit of darkness but couldn't stop the descent.

She woke again, this time in an ambulance, the siren wailing above her own wailing. Strapped to a gurney, she flailed and called for police and search and rescue, or the fire department, anybody, between yelling to stop, stop, the boy on the bridge.

A woman constable materialized and assured her that even now people were looking for the boy. Nobody else had seen him on the bridge, but they would do whatever was necessary to find him. The paramedic checked her wrists and mumbled something to Cait, but the words made no sense. The constable shook her arm, but her words became faint and far away.

21: May: No Body

When Cait awoke, sun slanted in the window, and a clock on the wall said 10:30. *Nathan!* Cait levered upwards, which pulled the IV stuck in the back of her hand. Pain shot along her arm and into her head where lights, like in the arcade, lasered back and forth. She lay back down.

I'm going to throw up.

When the nausea passed, she sat up deliberately, keeping her hand flat on the mattress. Before she could shout or find the call-button, a nurse flipped back the curtain around her bed.

"Good morning. You have missed breakfast, but I'm sure I can get you some toast and juice, if you like."

"I don't like," said Cait, "I need to know about Nathan."

"Can't help you with that, but there's a grumpy looking gal in a uniform waiting to talk to you."

The uniform came in a few moments later. The bags under her eyes explained her grumpiness and croaking introduction.

Constable something, Cait only half-heard her name, told her they had no idea who the boy was, and in fact had no idea who she was.

"Your bag or purse must have gone missing in the kerfuffle on the bus, so no ID. You conked out–sorry, you became unconscious before you could give me names," she said. "And all night they searched the bridge, the riverbanks, and the river, but nobody has been found."

"His name is Nathan. My name is Caitlyn Lee. I'm the school counsellor. I must call the school. And his mother." Cait, disregarding the limitations of her hospital gown and the tether of the IV, swung her legs out of bed. "My phone, I need my phone."

That too was gone with the bag, but the constable, relenting in her peevishness, offered hers. Cait's trembling fingers tapped the school's number, and Jen put her through to Art Kinney.

"It's about Nathan, have you heard from his parents?" her shouted inquiry was answered with a pause.

"Nathan is in class," Art said. "I would really have appreciated a call if you weren't coming in today."

Nathan was in school? Cait mumbled something about banging her head, being in the hospital, and just waking up. She was awake, wasn't she? This wasn't a dream?

"Oh, well maybe take the day."

"I'm fine. I'll be there as soon as I can get discharged." Where were her clothes? In that closet?

"But we need to discuss Nathan," Art continued. "He's here today but is leaving. I spoke to his mother, who said that next week Nathan will change schools."

"But, but, the only other high school is on the other side of the river." Cait wished her throbbing brain would keep up.

"Yes, certainly." She saw the moustache-rubbing at the other end of the call. "Closer to their home. They moved a while back but thought it best to keep Nathan in this school. That's changed now, especially after some incident on the bridge yesterday that tied up traffic for hours. I guess Nathan felt well enough for hockey after being sick yesterday morning. And," continued Art, "on the recommendation of the shrink, his father has forbidden the arcade and all video games until the end of the school year. He's also confiscated Nathan's Xbox."

Cait brought the phone down and stared at it in her lap, then placed it in the outreached hand of Constable Whomever.

"So the young man isn't missing? Correct?"

"No. He's in class."

"But you're sure you saw somebody on the bridge?"

"I did see. I'm just not sure they were there."

The constable lifted her brows and her cheek pulled sideways. Not quite a smile. "We'll keep checking just to make sure. I'll go now, Miss Lee," the constable slid her phone into her pocket and shut her notebook.

R. Rigsby

"You'll let me know if, if, they find anybody?"

"Sure." The constable's shoulders dropped. "And I'll see if we can find your bag and phone."

Even to her own ears, Cait's voice sounded small and contrite. "Thank you."

22: May: Explanations

Cait fell back on her pillow and blew through her lips. She shut her eyes but when she opened them, the angle of the sun in her room had changed and she realized she had slept.

"Miss Lee?"

"Nathan!" Cait sat up. Carefully, remembering the IV, and at the same time wondering when she could have it removed so she could leave and…but here was Nathan right in front of her. "Nathan," she said again, knowing she sounded like a disembodied echo of herself, "you should be in school, why are you here?"

"Ravi told me you were here. He was in trouble again. He was outside Kinney's office and overheard everything." Nathan looked at the fold of the bed curtain he gripped and dropped it. "I had to see you."

"Ah, you have company." Cait and Nathan jumped as a middle-aged man poked his head around the curtain and looked past Nathan's shoulder at Cait. "Hello. I'm Dr. Rice. You're looking a lot perkier than when I saw you earlier."

"I need to leave here. I have a job to go to."

"I understand." He looked at Nathan. "Would you be so kind as to give us a moment?"

Nathan started. "Yeah, sure…"

"Don't leave yet," Cait said, sitting up. Too quickly. The room spun.

"No, I'll just go down the hall."

Cait lay back. The face of Dr. R…somebody melted and then coalesced. She shut her eyes, but not before catching the doctor's worry lines.

"Now then," he said, "I would love to send you home, but if you could hang around for a bit, you will have an MRI this afternoon. Deal?"

Cait opened her eyes. The doctor's face stayed in one shape, and he had resumed his professional expression of bland empathy.

She nodded. Sure. An MRI sounded great. Was Nathan still in the hall?

Dr. Rice saluted with two fingers and Nathan's face instantaneously appeared. Had she slept for thirty seconds?

Nathan opened his mouth, but with sudden clarity, Cait blurted, "Nathan, were you on that bridge last night?"

He looked at his shoes. "Yes. It's no big deal, Robbie and I have crossed on it before. I told him about my dream a while back. Yesterday, he said it might help if I just stood on it a while. And looked over. To see how it felt. Our house is on the river, so it's easy to get there. I didn't know you were on the bus and saw me."

"Nobody else saw you. I wasn't sure it was the real you I saw." Cait put a palm over her eyes.

"I'm sorry I scared you."

"I'm sorry about telling Mr. Kinney and getting Dr. Calder involved. And Dr. Benjamin. I've had time to think about your visions, and everything. We could have kept it between us for a while–at least talked it through first."

"It's okay," Nathan held up both hands, "I've thought about this too. You had to do your job."

Cait shook her head. Had she really done her job? "How's it going with Dr. Benjamin?"

"Better this time. He asks me a lot of questions about my dreams, my visions. I see a lot of stuff, but I guess not all of it happens."

"What about my dentist and Mr. Kinney and Miss Feenwell's fire?"

"Miss Feenwell is burning something all the time, so maybe that wasn't really a prediction. And maybe because I go to the same dentist, and they always call the morning before, I somehow knew they would call. I don't know. And Miss Feenwell likes me. She wouldn't go through with her report."

"But the other dream? About the bridge? I had that one too."

"You did?"

"Yes, but like you I couldn't tell if it was me, or, or somebody else…it was scary…so real. I was falling."

"Falling? Did you jump?"

"I don't know. I don't think so." Then she laughed knowing it sounded demented but not able to stop herself. "Things haven't been that bad."

Nathan's brows rose. He opened his mouth, closed it. His shoulders slumped. "I guess I haven't helped that, have I?"

"Alright, young man, I heard my patient had a visitor. But you know it's not visiting hours and this lady needs her rest." The nurse, although sounding officious, smiled. "You have one minute." She bustled away.

Cait lost whatever train of thought she was on, but another crossed her mind. "Did you have the dream last night? After being on the bridge yesterday?"

"No. Maybe it helped after all. Can I come back later? So we can talk about your dream?"

"Not later. Maybe tomorrow." The nurse was back.

Cait pouted. That woman popped up like a jack-in-the-box.

Nathan looked at her and blinked. "I should go," Nathan said, but didn't move.

Cait rubbed her eyes with her non-tethered hand. MRI? Why? The doctor hadn't explained. Did it have something to do with the cross-firing in her brain?

But at least Nathan's explanations kind of made sense. She dropped her hand. The bird. Crow.

"What about the bird? The crow. That hit my window? How did you know that would happen?"

Nathan rolled his shoulders, and his hands found his jacket pockets as he stepped back. "Well that's the thing. Maybe I saw that crow outside. Maybe it was sick. I might have just guessed it was going to smack into the window. And it did. Freaked me out too. I like crows and I'm sad it died. I haven't told Dr. B about that."

Cait closed her eyes and when she opened them, Nathan was gone.

23: May: That's It

The nurse lifted the tape that held the IV in Cait's hand.

"Deep breath, now," she said, "this won't take a sec."

Cait lay back and breathed consciously. Why had she been so flippant about her dream? Laughing for goodness' sake. She had worried Nathan. But at least she was sure the bird hitting her window had been a coincidence, eerie and shocking as it was. Nathan admitted as much.

"Your young visitor seems nice. A relative?"

"No. A student at my school. Where I work. I'm a counsellor. He's been having some troubles."

"Don't they all at that age? Everything is so dramatic, so tense, so *deep*. It's a wonder any of us get through those years. I'm sure he'll be fine."

"Yes. I'm sure too." And she was. Was she also suffering from an overabundance of the dramatic? Too close in age to be properly objective?

"There you go, now, pesky IV gone, but you will have an MRI later this afternoon. You are jumping the queue." The nurse glided off through the door.

Before Cait finished poking at her lunch, she was loaded into a wheelchair and taken to the imaging labs on the first floor. She hadn't realized she was on the second floor. She had never had an MRI, but as soon as she saw the cylinder they were about to shove her into, she tensed.

"I don't think I can do this," she said, sitting up and reaching a leg to the floor.

"Whoa, there, it's okay. Lots of people feel claustrophobic," said the technician. "We can give you a few minutes."

She was parked in the waiting area like a misplaced parcel. Why this sudden sensation of claustrophobia? That had never happened before. She had never had any phobias about anything, and for that matter, had never had nightmares. Many dreams like most people had, but none so vivid or as disturbing as those she had had lately. Was it the job? The newness of it all? The disorientation? But she had gone to two different universities and had had no trouble reorienting herself to new geography, new timetables, new people. But none of those people were Nathan.

An hour later, after focussed deep breathing, she visualized the machine. It was just a big doughnut and took seconds. She called the technician.

"Let's get this done," she said.

Later, Cait stared at her supper plate. Her head felt like a cannonball and about as dense. She propped it up with an elbow on the tray-table and toyed with the mashed potatoes.

"That's all there is to it."

That's what the technician had said after the MRI. She pushed the table away and lay back on the pillow.

She didn't mean to drift off to sleep, but her head felt better with her eyes closed, and really there was no reason to worry over Nathan. He was getting the care he needed and that morning he had sounded a lot more rational than her. *That's all there is to it.*

She was on a bridge, black, emptiness all around, and then she was falling, falling, into the water below....

24: May: The Right Bridge

Silent shrieking in her head, heart galloping, blood pulsing in her ears, she stretched out an arm to grab Nathan. *Stop screaming, I'm coming.*

She awoke with a spasm that shook her bed. She was the one screaming. The whole floor must have heard her. She braced one side on her elbow, panted and gulped for air. In the dark. She had slept well into the night. Her screams weren't real, they were in the dream, another dream. Her heart slowed to a trot instead of a gallop. She pushed herself upright and sat on the edge of the bed.

It was a dream, wasn't it? She should feel safe, secure, knowing that as horrific as it was, the feeling would pass. But she didn't feel safe. Not at all. In fact, on recalling where she had been, her heart picked up its pace.

It had been a vision. Nathan. He was on the bridge. She knew it. This time he needed her. The lights in the hall were dimmed. Still dark outside and quiet on the ward. No nurses padding on rubber soles or murmurs of a hospital waking up. No breakfast aromas, no rattling medical carts coming to distribute morning meds.

R. Rigsby

Cait slipped off the bed and opened the closet. She pulled on her clothes but couldn't find her shoes. Who needed shoes? The hospital-issue grippy socks would do. She found the stairs to the ground floor and the main entrance. Which was locked. She would have to go out through Emergency. She walked down the hall as if she were at work checking for students who should be in class. In any case, anybody who might have paid her any attention, or noticed her choice of footwear, was busy attending to the contents of an ambulance. Lights flashed and people shouted. Cait stepped aside for paramedics shoving a gurney through the door.

She strode to the far reaches of the parking lot where she sat on the curb to catch her breath and ease the blood pounding in her brain. It was only a bump on the head, wasn't it? Although that doctor this–Rice?–hadn't been by to tell her the results of the MRI. She had no phone, no purse, but she knew where to find the bridge. And Nathan.

Traffic was minimal, and she met no other pedestrians on her way downhill through the centre of town. The intersection lights all flashed red. Rush hour, such as it was, was hours off. Cait shaded her eyes against the blinking. It had sprinkled a few hours before. April showers bring May flowers? No that was wrong. It was already May. The wet pavement smell was nothing like flowers.

A man hunched in a doorway. From under a blanket, he watched her progress. He stared, but neither called nor got up. She quickened her steps, one sock flapping, toward the river and, yes, the trestle! It would be the train bridge, of course. That's what she saw in her dream. Nathan had too.

Cait crossed multiple tracks on the other side of the old train station which was now a museum and coffee shop. Light from the single fixture over the door reflected on the wet rails. One train line ran straight on down the river, but the other crossed to go up the valley on the other side of town. She found the right set of tracks and followed toward the river and the trestle.

Pitch black down here. Trains didn't need streetlights. She ignored the shivers that ran up the backs of her arms and marched toward the bridge, stepping from tie to tie, avoiding the gravel that was rough on her now bare feet. Where were her socks? Suddenly the black spaces between the ties weren't dark gravel-covered ground, but black, empty air. She paused and looked down. She couldn't see the water, but she knew that now, with the beginning of the spring melt, it ran swift and deep. She smelled it. That combination of dank weeds, wet wood where the waves slapped the pilings, and a taint of creosote. Was this the right bridge? Why was this so confusing? There were other bridges. She stopped.

She looked up at the whoosh of a few cars moving on the well lighted span above her. Yes. There was the vehicle bridge. She was on the right track. She giggled at her little joke and swayed with sudden dizziness. This was the right bridge. She stepped along the ties. Just like walking from stone to stone on a garden walk. Only look where you want to put your foot, not at the gaps. She stopped.

There were no guardrails, but every few meters there were upright wooden posts, maybe for the convenience of track inspectors. She had no idea but gripped one and peered ahead into the gloom. Dawn wasn't far off–a slice of vanilla sky hung above the hills to the east, silhouetting a flight of birds.

"Nathan!" she called.

25: May: The Plunge

Cait staggered forward. One step at a time. Just look at the ties, not the gaps. She reached another post and clung to it. Was she lost in this void? Which way was back? Agoraphobia swirled through her mind but the air around her pressed like black velvet in a casket. Not that she had ever been in a casket. Such silly thoughts at a time like this.

"Nathan!" she called again. "Are you here? Wherever you are, stay there. It's Cait Lee. I'm coming!"

"Miss Lee! You stay put. I'm coming to help you."

Nathan was coming to help her? That was silly too. She was the helper, not the helpee.

Cait abandoned her post and stepped forward, as Nathan must have been doing. A movement or sound alerted each to the possibility of collision. Cait stopped mid-step then pulled back to the tie she had been on, and Nathan did the same. Two spaces and one tie between them. Cait wobbled, one hand groping for a post, but knowing it wasn't there.

"Nathan! I'm so glad I found you. I know why you are here but come with me now. It'll be okay."

"I had a dream," Nathan said. "I had to come here."

"So did I. But we can fix whatever is scaring you, I'm sure of it. There's no need for you to try to end it this way. Think of your parents."

"End it? Me? That wasn't my vision. I saw you falling. Maybe it was you I saw right from the beginning."

"Me?" Cait saw Nathan more clearly now. He looked as he always did: hair in his eyes; eyes that were wide open in fear, not for himself, but for her.

Dawn had come on rapidly, almost as rapidly as the flight of birds she had seen in the distance. Black specks against a platinum sky grew wings and beaks. They flapped downriver toward them. And cawed. Crows. Hundreds of them. They flew under the car bridge and came straight at the mid-span place where Cait and Nathan balanced.

Nathan wasn't looking at the crows, but Cait was. She threw her hands up and stepped back. Onto nothing. She dropped between the ties, her palms and nails scraping rough greasy wood, and screamed.

She was going to die. She saw the water, oily black. It would be freezing. She didn't swim that well if the splat in the water didn't kill her.

But she wasn't falling. Her hand was caught. It was Nathan. He had her wrist.

"Don't kick, don't struggle! Just let me pull you up slowly."

And he did. With that wiry strength of youth, he hauled her up and she lay clinging to a tie. The whole trestle tipping over. No it wasn't, it was her reeling head.

"Come on," he said, "let's get off this bridge. I hear a freight downriver."

Cait got up on her knees, then onto her feet. She allowed Nathan to guide her step by step to solid land. From far away a police siren echoed the screaming in her head. She was safe. Why the hot wire in her brain?

"Hallooo," a voice came out of the translucent dawn, followed by a solid form. Dave Grewal.

Cait looked at Nathan.

"I called Dave before I left home to look for you. I told him I was going to the bridge. I was worried about you, from something you said yesterday. But let's just tell other people that I called you."

26: August: Crow Warning

Dr. Benjamin stepped out leaving Cait, lounging in the plushy armchair by the window, to contemplate their discussion of the past hour. This was their last session together and school would start in two weeks. She stretched and yawned. She might have a nap when she got home. Enjoy it while she could, but it would be great to get back to work. She looked out at the August afternoon. Dr. B's third floor office had a nice view of the park where a family of crows squabbled over something they had found in the grass. She assumed they were a family. Some of them assumed the begging position of young birds.

She and the good doctor, among other things, had discussed crows. Or rather her feelings about them. The subject came up when he asked her to describe what happened on the bridge. She said she fell because the crows had startled her which led to at least fifteen useless minutes on the discussion of crows. To end it, she redirected the conversation to the book with the crow on the cover, which she had finished, and how prophetic that the protagonist also had a brain tumour. Maybe the book was trying to tell her something, not the crows. Dr. B 'hmmmmed' and made notes. She just wanted to get back to her life.

She would never plod the 'treadmill of death' again. She had escaped with that phone message in January. She hadn't anticipated some of the effects of that escape, including that last event on the trestle, crows notwithstanding. And what came afterwards.

The man she saw in the doorway, on her unsteady trek through town in floppy socks, had followed her and saw her go onto the trestle. He thought the worst and called police. She never found out who he was or how he had found a pay phone or if he had a cell phone. The police had called the ambulance, just in case, and that turned out to be a good thing.

That night after walking, or staggering, off the bridge with Nathan, Dave Grewal had taken one look at her and would have dialled 911 if police and paramedics weren't coming across the tracks. Something about her eyes, he said later, confirmed by the MRI.

It had been a small tumour, operable and benign fortunately, but big enough to press on her brain. The specialist had words for her on why she hadn't sought medical attention sooner, because of the headaches. But the pressure in her head could have messed up her judgement, causing her to ignore the symptoms. Could it have caused other things?

Later, when she had to explain her behaviour to authorities, including police and a social worker, she pointed out that the incident on the bridge was simply a case of a caring individual (her) who was under the stress of concern for a troubled student who had called her. That she hadn't called others for help was an error in judgement, possibly aggravated by the undiagnosed tumour.

After the surgery and eventual discharge, she had insisted on recovering in her apartment, rather than go home to be smothered in care. Her parents took up residence for the first few days, then alternated. The smothering came to her. On their last visit, they brought Firefly, who now dwelt in a large box stall at the stable. She and Pokey had become good friends. Too funny.

Last month, she, with Dave as support, had met with the school board. Art Kinney had wanted to fire her, but she had argued that she wasn't suicidal and there was nothing to prove that she was. She offered her doctor's report, and the board was convinced that she was cured. It probably helped that Sam Goode had officially retired. His wife, and his doctor, had insisted. Art Kinney had remained recalcitrant but accepted the inevitable.

However, as a compromise, Cait had agreed to counselling with a psychiatrist. There weren't many such specialists in this town, so like Nathan she was seeing Dr. Benjamin. A conflict of interests? Nobody else seemed to think so. Apart from his obsession with crows, her appointments with the good doctor mostly covered how she felt about her recovery and whether she was still as keen on being a school counsellor as before.

Teagan had come up last week. It was her turn to cope with a lumpy couch.

"What about the shop?" Cait had asked when Teagan dropped her backpack on the floor.

"Slow time of year. My one and a-half staff can handle it. What about your head? Tell me everything from the beginning."

"The beginning starting when?" Cait laughed. "I had brain surgery, I feel great. No headaches, no fireworks behind my eyes."

And no indecision. That part wasn't anything to do with the tumour. She woke up from the surgery knowing the job she wanted now more than ever was in this town in the interior, hot summers and freezing winters and all. Maybe one day she would move back to the big city on the coast, but for now there were students here who needed her. And maybe somebody else.

Teagan had left after three nights, somewhat satisfied that Cait could survive on her own.

"I'm better every day, T, not so tired. I cook, I eat, I have a job to go to in two weeks," Cait had told her. "I'm cured one hundred percent."

Dr. Rice, and the latest MRI proved it. There was no tumour.

Which was why the vision that came to her after Teagan left was a shock. It was a mild episode, not at all as intense as others, more of a movie-frame-on-loop showing something she should do.

She had called Art Kinney and asked to meet him in his office, although he was still on vacation. It was the first time they had spoken since the meeting with the school board when he had said she should be fired.

"Cait!" he said, when she tapped on the door jamb. As usual, he had been frowning into his computer screen. "Please, come in. Are you feeling better?" He stood up and positioned a chair for her.

Cait had nodded, alert. Was he glad to see her? The smile was a real smile. He hadn't rubbed his moustache.

"I feel great." Cait sat on the edge of the chair. "And I'm looking forward to school starting."

"That's good. I too am looking forward to this year. I wanted to talk to you, and I would have called you if you hadn't called me. You'll be happy to hear that the school board has found us a new vice principal."

Cait waited. Did he really say 'us'?

He picked up a pencil and held its ends between both index fingers. He gazed at the pencil, then smiled at her with a real smile, not the bared teeth grimace.

"I want you to know that I'm glad you will continue to be our counsellor. I may have been over considerate of Sam, and not given you due support. He told me that he wanted to retire last fall but didn't want to abandon me with neither a VP nor a counsellor."

Cait suppressed a sigh. Well, he had said everything she had wanted to say to him. She smiled. "You've had some challenges this past year."

"It has been a year like no other, but every school term has its bumps."

"Maybe it's the bumps that keep us here."

Art sat back with his hands behind his head and laughed. "Yes, indeed."

Cait had paused on the steps on her way out. Art might not be quite as much of a bully as she had thought. Thinking of him as pompous with an overinflated ego might not be fair. Nor constructive. The 'Pink Shirt Day Revisited' had gone well. He had allowed the kids to run it, as she had asked. Ravi and Robbie and Nathan had become good friends. When she had become well enough for visitors, Dave had kept her up to date on school news.

He had resigned and taken a job at the other high school, because, as he had admitted to her, he hoped to see more of her. Socially, as he put it. If she wanted to. He hadn't said so, but she considered that he would be able to keep an eye on Nathan in his last year of high school. She was glad of that.

"Ooooh," Teagan had said. "You better keep me up on how this goes. And about that Nathan kid too."

"He's doing well. He and his parents brought me doughnuts in the hospital," she had told Teagan. His mother said she was sharing them with me because

Nathan is always buying them for her. "His father changed jobs and will be home every night."

Cait stretched again in the big comfy chair. Where was Dr. Benjamin? His secretary had interrupted their session in a flap–something about an urgent call from a distressed parent. Nathan's mother? Or father? Why would she think so? It wasn't likely now.

Cait turned her head to look through the window at the bright blue day above the park.

She didn't see the crow coming, just the explosion of black feathers as it hit the glass and another vision exploded in her mind.

"Nathan!" Cait leapt to her feet and ran for the door.

27: August: Two Hours Earlier

Cait got off the bus outside the old train station two hours before her appointment with Dr. Benjamin and glanced at her phone. Plenty of time for coffee with friends. She strolled around the corner to the front of the building. Dave and Nathan sat at a table outside the museum's coffee shop. Both jumped up.

"Cait!" they chimed together, then, "Sorry, I mean Miss Lee," said Nathan.

"You can call me Cait when it's just the three of us. And especially if you get me an iced mocha."

With drinks in place, they sat at the table, from where they had a good view of the trestle. Cait turned her chair although it placed her where the sun hit her full in the face. She blinked and pulled her hat down. What was it about the black angles of that bridge that sent prickly chills along her spine? Apart from having dangled underneath it?

Nathan seemed unperturbed. He gazed at the bridge while telling them about his sessions with Dr. B. Nobody could predict the future. Anything he had ever predicted before was either sheer coincidence or based on perceptive guesses. He said that is what he had agreed after many discussions.

"Dr. B says anybody can say anything about what might happen, but people only pay attention when their predictions come true. If nothing happens, nobody pays any attention. So he said." Nathan swept the lock of hair out of his face and stared at the trestle.

"Do you believe that?" Cait said.

"Nope. Not at all."

"I didn't think so."

"But it keeps everybody happy when I say so. And they don't treat me like a freak. Or weirdo, like Ravi used to call me. If my visions are a gift, I'll find a way to deal with it."

"I wish I could have done more to help you," Cait said.

Nathan looked at her with his odd half-smile. "You've been great. I don't know what would have happened if you hadn't come to our school when you did. I must have been the student in your first dream. When you were sitting on that bench."

Maybe it was true, but the details of that vision were now far away and fuzzy around the edges.

"You still have visions, don't you?"

Nathan shrugged. "Don't you?" He twitched his usual half-grin. His eyes gleamed, but his brow remained unfurrowed. He looked at Dave, then back at Cait.

Cait thought of her last vision. Marching into Art's office and straightening him out on a few things. It hadn't gone exactly as she had seen, but she had had the vision. She should practice Nathan's shrug. He seemed to have it down to an art form.

"Dave and I talk about this a lot," Nathan said. "I think I will always have visions. It might be something given to me."

"You've got a few more days of freedom before school. Any plans for this afternoon?" Dave said, lifting his glass to Nathan.

"Robbie and Ravi are at the arcade. I might meet them there. Then there's something I need to do."

He smiled at Cait and Dave, then looked again at the bridge.

R. Rigsby

28: August: Crow Summons

Cait flashed through Dr. Benjamin's reception room. She caught sight of the secretary's open mouth and a glimpse of Dr. B in his office, rubbing his forehead and holding the phone to his ear.

"Miss Lee…wait, Dr. Benjamin would like to finish your session…"

Cait ignored her and, not bothering with the elevator, clattered down two flights of stairs, already puffing. Man, so out of shape. She jogged the two blocks to the museum. Dave's car was still parked in front and Dave called from across the street where he stood holding a bag of groceries. She waved and pointed but carried on and panted around the corner to the front of the building. She stopped and huffed, hand on a planter for support, and stared out to the trestle where a dark figure stood. Nathan.

A crow circled below the bridge where Nathan looked down at the water. It cawed as it dipped and flapped up to the bridge level, then dipped again. Nathan's last words at the coffee shop came back to her. *Something he needed to do.* He reached for one of the upright posts and leaned over the side of the bridge. His other hand gripped the handles of a small box, but Cait only saw his surrender to the call of the crow.

"Nathan!" she screamed and ran.

29: August: Death by Crow

Cait wiped her streaming eyes and blew her nose. It was a lovely service. Dave beside her surreptitiously handed her another tissue. She didn't catch the celebrant's closing comments, but when everybody stood, the relief made her knees weak. It was over. Mercifully.

With Dave's hand on her elbow, she rose and followed the people in their pew seeing only a bleary wash of dark suits and dresses. Outside, on the steps and lawn, mourners gathered in small groups of nodding heads and low voices. Art Kinney left a group and joined them, leaving Mrs. Kinney to console a petite woman in a navy dress whose wide hat and dark glasses didn't disguise her blotched face and shaking shoulders.

"I couldn't believe my ears when I heard what happened on the trestle, Cait."

"Nothing '*happened*' Art, as you well know." Dave said, in a low-level growl. "Nathan was on his way home. With doughnuts for his mother. You can't blame Cait for–"

"I know, I know, and I don't...." Art rubbed his moustache and looked to where a man brought a chair for the grieving lady. She sat and leaned forward. Mrs. Kinney patted her back.

Cait stifled a sneeze and blew her nose.

"So sad," Art said to Dave and patted Cait's arm, as if patting was the ultimate in consolation techniques. "Who would have thought this would happen? He was never the same after that business with the crow."

Cait nodded and gave her nose a final blow. The hall had been filled with flowers. Asters, maybe? And carnations? She had no idea she was allergic to flowers as well as hay. She looked up to see a tall figure approach and smiled.

"I'm so glad you came," she said.

"Of course." Nathan flicked his half-grin, then sobered. "I'm really sad about Mr. Goode. He always meant well."

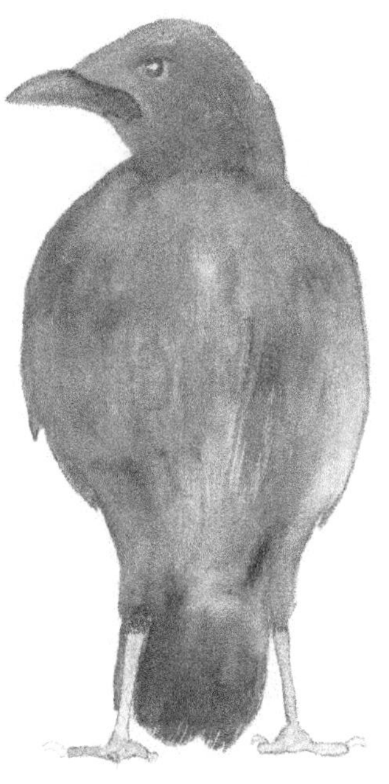

Acknowledgements

No writer works in a vacuum, and I have many people to thank for making *Death by Crow* become a reality. From the critiques of my writer group, the comments of my beta readers, and the advice of my editor, this story evolved and grew wings. I thank them all.

Death by Crow was almost finished when I read *Crow* by Amy Spurway, and I had an 'aha' moment. Cait reads books from the shop on her breaks–why not Amy's *Crow*? It was a perfect fit, and I thank Amy, not only for her amazing writing, but for her kind advice to seek permission from her publisher to reference *Crow* in my book. This was generously given, and I am grateful for the support from both Amy and Goose Lane Editions.

Which brings me to my gratitude for family, including mothers and sisters, and Grant is ever my staunchest supporter and believer. Our kids are the best, and our grandkids, who I hope will one day inherit, if not a love of writing (they are all readers), then the belief that it is possible to do anything they decide to do.

About the Author

Rosemary lived her childhood and teen years in logging camps and small towns on Vancouver Island. Years later, she discovered the outlet of writing. This led to a biography, followed by a travel memoir and three novels. Rosemary usually writes at her desk with a view of the Urban Fir, but her couch and kitchen table work too, as does any summer cabin with a view of a lake.